MW01715458

Death on the Dakota Prairie

By

Tom Wudel

PublishAmerica
Baltimore

First printing

ISBN: 1-60474-983-0
PUBLISHED BY PUBLISHAMERICA, LLLP
www.publishamerica.com
Baltimore

Printed in the United States of America

Chapter 1

As Dr. Calvin Downing's cart exited Seventh Street onto Dakota Avenue at a pedestrian pace, the methodical clomp, clomp, clomp of the horse's mammoth hooves on the cobblestone street was interrupted only by the mournful coo of a lone dove in the distance. "Calvin...hey Downing...I'm over here."

Downing, deep in his own thoughts on this early Friday morning, was startled by the sudden commotion. "Who's there?"

"Over here Calvin! Lord man, you almost ran over me! I thought you were coming by to visit."

"I'm sorry Frank, got a lot on my mind this morning I guess. How have you been?"

"Been doing just fine, I haven't seen you since lunch at the club last Friday. Now what could the good doctor have weighing on his mind so heavy he almost runs me down?" Judge Frank Acres and Dr. Calvin Downing could almost be brothers. Both men, tall and in their late forties, were successful professionals and leaders in the Sioux Falls community. The two men, teamed with Walter Wiseman, local brewery owner and one of the most powerful men in South Dakota, had helped build Sioux Falls, South Dakota into The Queen City of the upper Great Plains. Ruth Wiseman, Walter's ne'er-do-well' wife however, had a little drinking problem.

"I'm on my way over to Walter's house. He's been out of town for a few weeks and you know how Ruth gets," Downing bent his elbow and raised his arm to indicate she had been drinking.

Frank was concerned. "How bad is she?"

"Pretty bad, you remember that pogrom in Europe that's been in the news?"

"The one when Passover and Easter fell on the same Sunday?"

"That's the one Frank; Christians killed over a hundred Jews that day. Anyway, Ruth seems to think that it happened here, and, that it could happen again!"

"In Sioux Falls, surely she imagines these things."

"I know, I guess I shouldn't be so hard on her, you know her mother and father were killed in a Polish pogrom when Ruth was only eight years old? Her aunt raised her here in the States. She does worry me though Frank, last week she told me that her servant girl was trying to kill little Emmalena."

Frank rubbed the stubble on his unshaven chin. "I'm sure you told her that her Emmalena died over two years ago in that horrible flu epidemic."

"I told her, Frank."

"What did she say?"

"Nothing, she just walked over to that chair, you know, the one she has sitting in the middle of the parlor facing that portrait of the dead girl, sat down and cried.

"That is sad Calvin. What are you going to do with her?"

"Settle her down is about all I can do, I have some drugs to sedate her till Walter gets back in town tonight, and he handles her pretty well. You know Judge; I owe a lot to Walter Wiseman. He helped me get the hospital started twenty years ago, and you know we are adding another new wing! I would do anything for him……speaking of anything, I'd better get over to see what Ruth found to drink this time!"

"Have a good morning Cal, say; are you going to make our Friday lunch at the club? Maybe we should talk about getting Walter involved in that summer fest thing tomorrow night. It will be just like old times!"

Dr. Downing gave his horse a little giddy-up and sped off down the avenue to the Wiseman mansion. He was in a much better mood after talking to the Judge and his thoughts wandered, "June 1st, 1906 and it's Dr. Downing to the rescue, again. Whatever Ruth got a hold of to drink this time must have been bad; she usually waits till she gets up around noon to call me." He pulled a hanky from his vest pocket and wiped the perspiration from his brow, "this heat isn't helping any, and it's going to be a hundred degrees again today.

Downing eased his six foot two inch frame down from his buggy and tied the horse to the water tank beside the summer kitchen in the alley of the Wiseman house. Facing the morning sun, Calvin shaded his eyes with his hand to admire the twelve room Victorian mansion Walter had built for Ruth after their only child died two years ago. It was a fine, fine house Calvin thought as he made his way to the back door and reached for the door knocker to announce his arrival. "What is this, this door is open, Ruth never leaves a door unlocked when Walter is out of town, and she is very peculiar about that. Downing's eyes darted about. The only way this door would be unlocked is if someone left it open behind them as they left. Downing opened the door slowly, stepped into the mud room and paused to listen, he heard no sound. Two paces took him to the entrance of the laundry room on his left, he peeked in, nothing. But apparently the servant girl Walter hired several months ago didn't know how to use that new Mississippi washing machine; there were dirty clothes and sheets stacked all around. Four more paces took him into the usually tidy winter kitchen. Walter had spared no expense in building this house and the kitchen was no exception. Beautifully crafted oak cabinets from the north woods of Minnesota lined the walls and finely crafted granite counter tops were shipped in special from the Black Hills of western South Dakota.

Downing, getting more nervous with each passing second, crept through the kitchen, the wood floor creaking with each step. Empty beer bottles littered the counter tops. "There must be twenty, maybe even thirty empty beer bottles here, no wonder Ruth isn't awake yet. But where is that servant? Someone should be here!" Downing's hand slid over a wet spot on the counter and it startled him, as he jumped back, two or three empty beer bottles went over the edge and crashed to the floor sending thousands of pieces of glass everywhere.

"Damn it, I am such a klutz! He paused and listened . . . but maybe that will wake someone up around here. It didn't, no sound came from any of the twelve rooms.

"This is making me nervous, I can't lose Ruth on my watch, and I can't fail Walter!" He thought, hard, "Ruth sometimes sleeps it off in the parlor where the ventilation was better than upstairs." Downing crept down the hallway past the dining room to his left and the billiard room to his right…he tripped on something. "What the hell." The morning sun had not yet lit the hallway so Downing had to reach down and feel for what he stepped on. It was a wet towel. He picked it up and inspected it as best he could.

"I need more light."

Reaching the end of the hallway, he turned left into the parlor. Early morning sunrays dimly lighted the room. His first instinct was to inspect the towel and when he held it up, his worse fears were realized…blood! Downing just now felt his first real sense of fear, and anger.

"Ruth, are you in here!" A nervous man, Downing was having trouble focusing. He took a step towards the McKinley rocker over by the revolving bookcase in the corner of the room. Squinting in the semi-darkness, he realized she was not there. Having tried hard to avoid it, his eyes finally found the portrait of the dead Emmalena, painted just weeks before her death, "Damn that painting, her eyes just penetrate," Downing, looking up at the portrait, stumbled on something and landed on the Victorian day bed against the wall. It was Ruth, lying on the floor in the fetal position.

Downing pulled himself up, put his hands on his knees and studied her for a moment thinking she might be dead. Her shoulders moved once, then her left breast heaved as she exhaled…she was breathing! Downing reached down slowly and tugged on her night shirt, covering her exposed lower body. Then, slowly, he cradled the petite woman in his arms, turned, and gently laid her on the day bed that was probably her original target. Ruth opened her eyes, "Walter?"

"No Ruth, it is Calvin, Dr. Downing."

Ruth tried to speak but was weak and the dry cotton mouth that comes when a binge is over, caused her to wheeze when she breathed. "You rest Ruth, I'll get some water!" As Calvin rose and turned toward the hallway, he noticed something odd, there was a syringe lying on the parlor table. "Hmm...had Ruth tried to commit suicide? Is she drunk or doped up on something? What is going on here?"

Dr. Downing returned with a pitcher of water and purposely set it on the parlor table, the syringe was gone! He poured a glass of water and handed it to Ruth who had gotten herself up from the supine position. "Can you hold this or do you want me to?" Ruth nodded and reached for the glass with her left hand. "Drink it slowly." Downing queried "Ruth, the house is a mess; do you remember what happened here last night?"

Ruth drank the water and shoved the glass back to Downing for more. "The wind, the wind blows so hard here, everyday. Did you know doctor, when the Christians came to kill us Jews, my mother and father; they were riding on the wind. They were led by a Catholic woman warrior with a shield and a sword...she was here the last two nights. I fought her off!"

"Relax Ruth, you must relax." Downing held Ruth's hand and stroked her arm hoping it would calm her down. "We can talk about this later, you just rest." Downing thought Ruth would fall asleep and he could see if the servant girl was still in the house.

Mrs. Wiseman, nearly delirious, pulled herself forward to the edge of the couch, "She kept falling down, and I think she is very sick."

"Who is sick, your servant girl?"

"I had a lot to drink, I don't remember everything. I think she is dying."

"Dying, now what is going on here? Downing's relief that Ruth was alright was turning to anger. Something was very wrong. Not only was Ruth almost zombie-like when she spoke, she was doing the strangest things with her eyes! When she spoke, they almost bugged out of their sockets, she looked crazy. "She is upstairs, get me up and I will show you."

"I don't know Ruth, you are very weak."

"I can do this, I want to do this." She swayed to her right the first few steps but Downing steadied her. Together, they ascended the steep stairway to the upper bedrooms. It must have been a long climb for the doctor as Ruth smelled a lot like Walter's brewery. About half-way up Ruth stopped. "It was here that she fell. She fainted or something, and bounced all the way down thumping her head on every other step. It was horrible! Somehow, I got her back up these stairs to her room."

Downing was confused. Several scenarios scurried through his mind. "Was Ruth chasing the girl, or was the girl the Catholic woman attacker?"

"She is in there. Here is the key." Ruth stumbled as she tried to pick up the key laying on the floor. "I locked the door so she would not wander out again."

"Ruth, you go clean yourself up. I'll have a look at the girl."

In the twenty plus years Downing had been serving the good and bad citizens of Sioux Falls, he had never seen a human body so badly treated. If this poor girl had indeed fallen as Ruth had said, it must have been from the fifth floor of the First National Bank building. She was barely conscious and the bleeding from several cuts on her head had clotted and stopped. There were bruises on her face and arms, and her lower torso was in very poor condition. Upon closer examination, Downing noted the skin on both the right and left legs had been peeled away, scalded. There was a white, powdery substance on the open wounds. "What is this substance?" The doctor examined closer, "Lye, oh my God, someone poured lye on these wounds!"

"Damn it, what do I do now?" Downing knelt beside the bed to brace himself for the decision he would need to make. Doctors are trained to make quick decisions, life and death decisions, this is different. I must protect Ruth to protect Walter. "If I remember right, this servant girl is an immigrant from out on the prairie somewhere. She has no one here. If I am discreet and involve only the right people…."

A loud knock on the door startled Downing. It was Ruth.

"I did what you told me, I cleaned up some."

"Do you want to know how the girl is?" Downing asked sarcastically.

"I really don't care. She's one of them you know…Christian." Ruth was still somewhat distant when she spoke. "You have to help me."

"Help you! This poor girl is nearly dead from some mysterious means and I must help you? Does anyone else know about this?" Ruth shook her head indignantly…"Then you keep your mouth shut!"

Downing reached for his bag, the contents of which were morphine and heroine. He had thought he would need to sedate Ruth, but after seeing the syringe on the table, he didn't dare use it on her. This child needed help much more. Carefully measuring the dosage of morphine in his syringe, Dr. Downing found a vein in the child's arm, punctured it with the needle, and squeezed the plunger forcing the pain killer into her body. The girl went motionless, almost as if she was dead. Downing stepped back one pace, then another, "what a bloody mess, why didn't Ruth finish this he thought." Downing took the girl's arm and felt for a pulse. It was faint, but there was a pulse. He left the upstairs bedroom and found Ruth trying to wipe some blood from the stair railing. "You must listen carefully to me Ruth. I think the girl is going to die and I need to go get some help to move her. When your hired man gets here have him help you clean this place up and dress the girl carefully. I will return with an ambulance."

The ambulance from the Noble Funeral Home arrived at ten forty-five A. M. with Hubert Schnell on the reins, Downing met him out front. "Schnell, take the wagon around to the rear and bring your stretcher upstairs."

Schnell obeyed his command and within minutes, he and his helper had climbed the stairs to the sick room. His experience told him that every sick room was different, but this one was pathetic. There was a toilet wash stand in the corner, but it had no water in it. The bed was small and barren of sheets, the patient was nearly falling out of it. Why was the patient dressed so oddly? The temperature up here must be at least 90 degrees and the body was dressed in a large flannel night shirt tied up around the feet. The head was covered entirely by some kind of a bonnet. No, it was an apron, the strings tied up tightly around the neck.

"Is this a man or a woman?" Schnell asked.

Downing snapped. "What difference does it make, get a move on."

"I just want to know so I don't grab hold in the wrong place. That's all, sorry." Schnell didn't like Downing much. He was a rich doctor and always seemed to make a special effort to look down on the workers of the world. It's typical that he would be at a mansion like this one; it seemed that all the rich people in the city were patients of Downing at one time or another.

"It is a she," Downing answered almost apologetically, "A young woman who took sick and suffered a bad fall."

"Will she live? She appears to be in pretty bad shape." Schnell could only notice the size and shape of the girl. Young, five foot tall he guessed and before moving a patient he always guessed the weight so he knew what he was in for. "This one would be easy to move, she couldn't weigh more than ninety pounds."

"Not if we don't hurry up and get her down to your ambulance." Downing led the way down the stairs as the two men behind him carefully negotiated the steep, narrow stair way. As they descended, Schnell couldn't help but wonder why this rich girl was so poorly dressed. If they can afford this doctor, they should have a nurse or some kind of help.

After loading the patient onto the wagon a quick check of her pulse would determine whether this would be an ambulance or a hearse. The pulse was still faint but an ambulance it would be. "Go quickly Schnell, I'll follow you to the hospital."

Sioux Falls General Hospital was one of the finest medical facilities west of Minneapolis. Doctor Downing headed the staff of five physicians and thirteen full time nurses. As Hubert carefully placed the sick girl on a gurney and prepared to push her in, Downing went ahead to the front desk. "Jane, this patient is a friend of mine and I want the best possible care we can give her. Her name is Kaiser or something like that, and for the record, it is now, twelve o'clock sharp. I want her taken to room three where we can get a good look at what is wrong; find Nurse Ellie will you please."

"Do you want any of the other doctors to assist?"

"No."

Schnell delivered the girl to the third room down the emergency corridor and stayed with her until he had further instructions. "This girl can't be more than fifteen maybe? What could have happened to her?" Schnell was not being perverted in any way but had to look further at this mysterious girl. He lifted the blanket covering her legs. "My God, the skin is gone!"

"Schnell, what the hell are you doing?" It was Downing. "You are not a doctor! Get out of here, now!! Nurse! Nurse, get in here!" Dr. Downing was furious and Schnell was gone in a hurry.

Ellie Rumbolz, General's lead nurse arrived as ordered, "Look Doctor Downing, her arm, it moved, I tell you she moved! That is good!"

"Maybe to you, but experience tells me it is not. The more she moves, the more she loosens the bandages and that leads to bleeding. I think we should sedate her so she will rest without rolling about. Hand me my bag please nurse.

"You're bag is not here doctor."

"It must be. I always keep it close by...Oh; I must have left it at the front desk when I checked the girl in. Could you get it for me? I will keep the patient stable while you do."

The nurse followed her instructions and within a minute or two was back in room three.

"You have been a great help to me nurse. Now, I will give this young woman a nice shot of morphine so she can rest and heal. After she has quieted down we must change the bandages I put on at the house. Then, clean up those legs as best as you can. We must try and prevent infection if we can. Nurse, if you can check on her every hour or so, I will return around four, she should show signs of improvement by then."

The severely beaten girl did not. On Friday afternoon June 1st, the poor immigrant girl from Parkston, South Dakota died. Nurse Ellie was at her side.

Hubert Schnell was still on duty when the call came in so he hurried to the hospital thinking it could be the girl he took in this morning. He was right. This time he got a good look at her. He had seen many expressions on faces of the dead, but none touched him like this one. She had apparently suffered great pain and showed none of the signs of the relief death should offer. A look of quiet innocence seemed to be pleading for an answer for her torture! This time Schnell did not keep quiet.

"Dr. Downing, you pronounced this girl dead. But I will not take her to the morgue. The police should be called!"

"What are you talking about man?" Downing was in no mood.

"This body seems to be in very poor condition is all I am saying." Schnell was taking a big chance.

"She had diabetes and vertigo and died as a result of it. That is what happened. Now get her out of here." Downing was losing patience.

Schnell stood his ground. "All I am saying is that in cases where the body is in such poor condition the police may want to take a look into it. Shouldn't there be an autopsy?"

Downing snarled. "You look here you little ass-hole, I have had about enough today! The girl is dead, I signed the death certificate. Once again, she died of diabetes Mellitus, typhoid fever and anemia. We could not save her and if you continue to give me shit about it, I will call your boss and tell Denton that his little piss-ant driver thinks he is a doctor and a sheriff, and because of that, Noble Funeral Parlor will get no more business from this doctor or this hospital!" Downing was shouting now. "Is that what you want?"

Schnell knew his place. "No Sir."

"Then do your job! Tell Denton I will be by later to tell him where to ship the body. I have to go back to the Wiseman house to find that out."

It was nearly six o'clock when the doctor arrived at the Wiseman house. Walter saw him pull up and waved him in. "Come in, come in my friend. It is good to see you Calvin. I was shocked when I got your call about Agnes. What a tragedy."

"I agree Walter; I did everything I could. How is Ruth?"

"Resting, I am not sure if she understands what happened. Oh where are my manners, would you like a drink?" Walter loved to entertain. An elegant man, forty-seven years old, he always had that youthful enthusiasm. Not tall, but large, his presence could dominate the room. "I was very fond of Agnes, she worked very hard, let's take our drinks on the veranda. What happened to her?"

"An old country disease of some kind, with all the immigrants coming here the last twenty years, I've seen several that kill quickly." Downing was being very careful not to incriminate Ruth in any way. "Denton is working on the dead girl now. My diagnosis is diabetes mellitus. It caused her vertigo which led to several falls. She was also suffering from anemia which all contributed to heart failure. You'll have to tell me what to do with the body."

"Yes, of course Calvin, I will write out instructions for you to give to Denton. Please, tell him I will pay for everything. Make it a nice casket, something simple."

"I understand, you said she was from immigrant stock. They will bury her, cry over her grave and in a few days forget about her and get on with their pathetic little lives."

Walter thought his friend a bit cold, "Calvin, are you sure there was nothing Ruth could have done to prevent this from happening?"

"I don't know Walter. I guess you know Ruth drinks a little."

"A little, you are being kind my friend. I know she drinks a lot! She is better when I am at home, but you know how much I travel. You are the doctor, what should I do?"

"Be discreet."

"What do you mean, be discreet?"

"There is a sanitarium in Sioux City, a good one. It is for people like you Walter, you know, people who can afford to be discreet. I have sent several patients there for recovery and they all have good things to say about the place. What do you think?"

Walter sat silently for a moment, then stood and put his hand on Calvin's shoulder. "I want to thank you for taking care of this for me; there will be a nice donation for that new wing at your hospital. I also like your suggestion about Sioux City, I have been dealing on buying a small brewery down there and this would be a great opportunity to visit Sioux City, discreetly of course! But for now, I hate to be short with you but I must put in a call to my friend Ben Miller in Parkston. If Ruth and I are going to Sioux City, I won't be able to get out to Parkston next week. Did you know I'm building a warehouse there Calvin?"

"No, I didn't, why Parkston?"

"To better distribute my beer, you see Calvin; most people think the next Indian lands that the government will open up to homesteaders will be west of Pierre. My contacts out there tell me it will be far south of there, probably closer to Marty Mission. Parkston is the perfect place for a warehouse filled with Wiseman beer. Those thousands of settlers will be thirsty, who knows, I may even build a brewery there in the future."

"You are a real thinker Walter, listen, I need to get back to Noble's parlor and finish this thing up. Oh, and when you talk to your friend out there in immigrant land, tell him the body will be shipped in a closed, sealed casket. The girl died of a mysterious disease and we cannot afford to have the body exposed."

Chapter 2

Saturday, June 2, 1906

"Beer me up Bennie, it's Saturday night in Parkston!" Gottfried Rausch, the bearded, portly Parkston depot master bellied up to the bar, turned, and slowly surveyed the early crowd at Ben's Place. About half the tables down the right side wall of the bar were full and the pool tables in the back of the room were all in use. "Been a dust eating day at the old train yard Ben, what you got cooking in back, wurst, some chislic maybe?" Gottfried, Gubby, as most folks called him, was always hungry.

"I got some of each, but it's not out back. You walked right past it. I just laid the meat out on the front sidewalk about an hour ago and let the sun cook it."

"Damn good idea Ben, must be a hundred degrees again today."

"Here you go Gub, the first Wiseman beer is on the house, that's what Walter tells me to do! What's new on the east side today?" Several locals who liked to get their news about Parkston gathered around to hear what Gubby had for them. Gubby always knew who came into town and from where or vice-versa, who left for where and with whom!

"Got a box in just before I left the depot; sent rush, over night." Gubby sat back smugly on his stool, eagerly awaiting the next question.

"What kind of box Gub?" Ben did the honors.

"It was a casket. A small pine box with the word QUARANTINE painted on it!" Several more long-neckers gathered around. Gottfried was on a roll. "SEALED CASKET; DIED OF DISEASE! Very mysterious, Gubby kind of let mysterioussss…slowly roll off his lips. Zach is over there now picking it up. You got another Wiseman beer Ben?"

"Coming right up, yea, we just saw Zach go by. What a sight. Those two black Trotters, shiny with that silver tack. They just dance in that fancy canter. And the hearse! Well, people are dying all over the place just to get a ride in that thing!"

"Doggone it Gubby, Who the hell was in the box and where did it come from?"

"Good question Leonard…Gubby took a long refreshing drink of cold Wiseman beer and smacked the mug down on the bar. The box came here from…."

"Sioux Falls would be my bet!"

"Goddamn it Ben, why you always got to steal my thunder. You weren't there. You don't know where it came from."

Ben leaned over the bar and asked a simple question. "Where did the coffin marked QUARANTINE come from?"

Gubby lowered his head a little, "Sioux Falls."

"A little louder Gottfried, they can't hear you in back!"

"SIOUX FALLS SOUTH DAKOTA, did everybody hear?" Lucky for Ben Gubby was a guy who could take a little ribbing.

"Ben…Ben, down here!" The voice belonged to Ben's long time friend Clifford.

"Yea, I'll be right there Cliff. Nick, get Gubby here another Wiseman. Ben turned and walked the thirty feet or so to the other end of his bar in his slow, easy gate, "you drinking or working tonight Cliff?"

"No drinks, all work tonight." Cliff could use a drink but his hotel-café across the street did a brisk business on Saturday night. "I might take you up on that drink later though."

"You all right Cliff? You look kind of pale."

"Did you hear about Agnes? She's dead Ben!"

"Yea, I know. Gubby down there is filling everybody in except he doesn't know who the body is. Walter called me earlier, said the body was shipped last night. That's how I knew."

"Walter called you huh? So what does he say happened? Walter Wiseman stayed at Cliff's hotel when he was in Parkston selling his beer, but Cliff wasn't as close a friend to him as Ben was.

"He's feeling pretty bad. He didn't even know she was sick until it was too late. He only got back to Sioux Falls last evening. He said he felt bad that the girl didn't have any family around when her end came."

"I am to Ben; I'm the one who got her that job. Hell, it was right here, last January. We were playing poker at that table over there in the corner. You remember don't you?"

"Yea, I remember. Let's see...Karl was there, Walter of course. You, me and Floyd, there were six, who else?" Ben thought hard. "It was Doc. I forgot about Doc Hughes. He was kicking our ass that night. You remember Walter? He doesn't like losing at anything and Doc kept rubbing him. So what about that night Cliff? What do you remember?"

"Just that Walter was complaining about his home life. You know how tough he has it in that big mansion he got in Sioux Falls. He asked how I get girls to work in my hotel. He said he can't find any good ones to clean house and wash clothes. I just told him I get immigrant girls to work for me because they work so hard and don't complain! I told him about Agnes and he wanted to meet her to see if she had any friends who would want to work for him. Well, one thing goes to another and he ends up hiring Agnes away from me. To be honest, it kind of pissed me off. Now all this, Agnes being dead...I just feel responsible somehow."

"What is going to happen is going to happen, Cliff. Gubby just said the coffin is marked disease. Agnes just got sick and she died from some bad thing. Clifford, when Walter called me, he asked me to help make some arrangements for the funeral. He's met John and Christine and knows that because they are not long here in America, they may need help with money. I guess what I'm trying to say Cliff, Walter is a good guy. He said he would pay for everything, and if anyone needs a room for a few nights while all of this happens, I should ask if you would help."

"I appreciate that Ben. I suppose it would be a good idea if I set a room aside for John. I can let him have the suite that Walter always uses when he stays here."

"Hey Bennie. . . get up here, Rothes coming up Main Street with the hearse."

It was a sight to behold. Unlike his dash to the depot to retrieve the body of a poor soul and return it to the sanctuary of his morgue, Zachary Rothe turned the return trip into an expression of respect. He slowed the pace of his Trotters to a walk and let people pay respects all along the four block journey. Death was common on the plains, all the churches in town had their own cemeteries that were filling up and even though the churches did not get along very well, they all had respect for perished souls no matter what denomination. This particular night was no different except that it was a Saturday night. The streets were lined with people who came into town after a hard week of toil and sold eggs, or cream. The men bragged about their crops, the first liar never had a chance. The women would shop for new and expensive garments or utensils that would make their life easier, and then buy only the things they needed to survive. So when the hearse passed by on this Saturday night, the polka band stopped playing, men removed their hats from their head, and women and children strained to catch a glimpse of whose body lay dead in that big, black hearse. The only sounds came from the shit shoveler who was cleaning the street and the barking dogs who didn't like the horses. The great black Trotters were oblivious to both, there mission was to carry this casket home, disease or no disease!

Tradition had it that family members would accompany the body on this four city block parade, this way the crowd got to know who the dead person belonged to. This evening, there was only one person at the side of the ominous black vehicle, a smallish man leading a rider less horse. A whisper in the crowd began to swell that meant no disrespect to the dead. "That's Henry Moss!"

"Who is Henry Moss?"

"Well Henry Moss is that horse trader that lives southeast of Parkston a couple miles. But he's just an old bachelor lives out there. What would he be doing with that dead body?"

Rothes Funeral Home was only a couple hundred feet from the St. Peter Catholic Church on the west end of Main Street. Zach Rothe backed the hearse up to the unloading dock and went inside to get a cart, Henry waited outside to help. The body was of course already embalmed and the casket sealed, so there was little to do in preparation for the viewing. According to Christian belief, Agnes's soul had already departed and her body was ready for eternal rest, free from further suffering. The pain would now fall on the shoulders of her family and friends. Gathered in the funeral parlor's sanctuary were Agnes's parents, John and Christine Kreutzer and her six year-old sister Grace. Others included Father Mullaney and family friend Henry Moss. It was a small group to share such a large amount of grief.

Father Mullaney broke the silence. "John and Christine, Grace, in a few moments our church bell will begin to toll. Each toll of that bell is an expression of respect for each year of Agnes's young life. If my memory is correct that would sixteen, am I right John?"

"That is right Father."

"This can be heart wrenching so I would ask you all to bow your heads in prayer, Our Father who art…." The first clang from the bell made everyone shiver and each subsequent clang brought louder sobbing, mostly from Christine.

Henry Moss thought to himself, "It is like God Himself is right above us whacking that bell!"

With Christine and Grace clinging to John for support, he too broke down in uncontrolled sobbing…after the Lords Prayer; Father Mullaney, a young Priest with a twinkle in his eye and an Irish tenor voice, pulled Zachary back into the shadows of the sanctuary. "There is something you should know about the Kreutzer family. Their faith in the Lord is incredible. Maybe more so than any other family I know. You see Zachary, in Russia; some years before they immigrated here, Agnes had an older sister, Sophie. Much older than Agnes, Sophie had become alienated from John and Christine and ran away to the big city to be with her lover. John told me Sophie was sixteen at the time. After a few months had passed without hearing anything from Sophie, they went to Odessa to find her. What they found out was that Sophie had been murdered by her lover. Stabbed several times and left to die in the street, alone!"

Zachary took a hanky from his pocket, wiped a tear from his eye, and made the sign of the cross across his chest. "God have mercy on the souls of Sophie and Agnes."

Henry Moss was the only one who saw Ben Miller and his daughter Madeline come in the front door. "Ben, I'm glad you came by, but the body is not ready quite yet."

"Sorry Henry, You know little girls, Madeline just begged to come down here just to catch a glimpse of her friend's casket. How are they holding up in there?"

"Those bells really tore them up. Me too I guess." Henry was still a little bit shaken.

"Listen Henry, just tell Zach and Father that Walter called me and feels real bad about this. He wants you all to know, how can I put this? Tell John not to worry about money. Walter has wired Cliff some money for rooms so they can stay in town close to Agnes."

"I'll tell him, I can take care of things on the farm. I'll see you down at the bar later, we can talk more about what else we can do to help."

"You bet. I need to get Madeline home, church comes early in the morning. Do you know when the funeral will be? Walter just said the doctors over there were concerned that they didn't know anything about this disease. They just thought the sooner the better."

"I don't know Ben; it won't be tomorrow, probably Monday morning."

The blue clear South Dakota sky was slowly and steadily turning into a picture perfect prairie sunset of red and orange. John spoke softly as his family climbed into the buggy Henry had brought around front. "Look at that sunset, Christine. God is welcoming Agnes to heaven. Oh, how Agnes loved sunsets. When you were on the big boat HORTENSE coming to America, she would stand on the deck and watch the sunset." Pulling Gracie close to him John continued. "Agnes would hold you Grace, and sing to you. She would sing lullabies until you fell off to sleep. Yah, Agnes loved the sunsets. We must promise to ourselves, all of us, that every time we see one, no matter where we are, we will say to ourselves, I remember you Agnes. I love you Agnes......we can go to the hotel now my good friend Henry Moss, it has been a long day."

The hours at Ben's Place were strictly enforced, the saloon closed when everyone had gone home or was passed out! It was about ten o'clock when Henry and Cliff walked in and this Saturday would be no exception. The two men tried to make their way toward the back of bar where Ben was but weren't having much success. Henry squeezed and ducked his way through and pulled up a stool but the much larger Cliff was stuck in the drunken Saturday night crowd, "Back up Cliff, come around behind the bar, and grab a couple bottles of Wiseman on your way down here!" Ben had secured a wide stool for his portly friend.

Ben wasn't German like most folks around here; he had just been passing through Parkston on his way farther south where other Bohemians were settled. He had some money in his pocket and intended to build a saloon down there, but when a wheel broke on his wagon, he just stayed in Parkston. Ben, six foot tall, and left-handed on the keg handle, moved slowly behind the bar, constantly watching his crowd for anything they might need. "You get the Kreutzer's settled in over there boys?"

Cliff had finally landed on his perch. "Yea, Henry brought the Kreutzer's up from the funeral home and we got them settled. We thought we would see how you were doing. Good crowd Bennie."

"Yea, it's been good, listen, our table back there is going to open up, let me get back there and clean it up. You guys come along, Floyd went home but Doc is delivering a baby, he should be here soon."

By eleven o'clock Ben had joined the group at the round table. Cliff, Doc Hughes, and Henry were all solemn in their private thoughts. Studying the half empty Wiseman beer bottle in his hand, Henry mused. "Agnes died in this man's home. What kind of a man is he?"

Cliff was just about to answer when…"Walter Wiseman is a great man!" Ben stood up and put his arm on Henry's shoulder. "When I started this saloon eleven years ago there were grasshoppers jumping all over the prairie, ate every thing in sight! Farmers were getting wiped out all over eastern South Dakota. Walter gave me credit on the beer I bought from him. I paid him for only what I sold. He carried me through that bad year."

Cliff was quiet but Doc spoke up. "A shrewd man, he didn't like to lose that's for sure."

"Damn straight Doc, I remember you that night last January when your cards were so hot they could melt the snow outside."

"Not that hot my friend, it must have been twenty degrees below zero that night! I have a little catching up to do on the beers here Ben, bring me a shot of schnapps will you?"

"That sounds good, bring us a round!" Henry enjoyed a cold beer but didn't drink liquor much.

"You sure Henry, I saw you the last time you had liquor, you didn't do to well."

"I'll be fine, just a shot or two."

Doc asked Henry a typical doctor question. "Why shouldn't you be drinking? You sick?"

"Nah, I'm alright. Ben's just worried about me because I told him once the only person I ever really loved was my father. He died when I was sixteen. I knew where he stashed his hooch and I drank it all the night he died, thinking it would help ease the pain."

"Did it?'

"That night it did! But I was sick for a week. I didn't like my ma much, so after I felt better I ran away and joined the army."

"The army doesn't take sixteen year old kids do they?" Cliff asked.

"They do if you can ride like I can!"

Chapter 3

Sunday June 3, 1906

Henry Weaver Moss celebrated his thirty-eighth birthday a month ago; you would think a man that age would know better. Last night, Henry figured if he went out and drank a dozen or so bottles of beer and chased them with that many shots of schnapps, this bad dream would just go away. The slobber from his German Shepard dog Heidi licking his face at six in the morning brought Henry back to some sense of reality! He rolled over to shoo her away. "Ding-dang it girl, I did it again. Gad I feel awful." Henry took inventory of his body and none of the reports were good. Head, gut and right buttocks all hurt. "Why would my butt hurt? Henry thought hard but couldn't come up with an answer."

Pulling his aching five foot five body up to the edge of his bed, Henry dipped a towel in the basin of water on the night stand. Wringing the excess water from the towel took almost all the energy he had. The cool soothing wetness soaked into his throbbing head as he wrapped the towel around it. Henry slowly stood to see if the dizziness was gone and he needed some water to wash away the mouth full of crap he tasted. He was, at least for the first few steps in that direction, a bit wobbly, then..."Out of the way Heidi, I got to get outside to the John!"

It wasn't a pretty sight, night shirt soaked with sweat, trying to get boots on feet that didn't want them on, just to get to the outhouse. But he made it, and as he sat upon his throne, he figured out why his butt hurt. His hat was lying on the floor; Henry must have spent some time in here during the night!

Moss had been a horseman for as long as he could remember. He grew up in Missouri the son of a domineering and fanatically religious mother, and an indifferent father who loved ponies, freedom and beer. As far as parents go, Henry preferred his father. When Weaver Moss, one of the original Pony Express riders out of St. Joseph, Missouri died unexpectedly in 1884, Henry, only sixteen, quit school and joined the army. Instinctively good with horses, he was a horseman for the renowned Seventh Cavalry for ten years before retiring and buying a farm in Hutchinson County, South Dakota. One hundred and sixty acres of prairie grass land along the banks of North Branch Creek in Section twenty-eight of Liberty Township. Bought and paid for with army paychecks, Henry enjoyed the good life of raising and selling horses. The days of the cow pony had disappeared years back, but Moss still sold riding breeds. His inventory of thirty to forty animals was a mix of plow horses and wagon drawers. Moss sold a lot of them, enough in fact to have paid for one of the finest houses in the county. The house, and a couple of barns large enough to stable his steeds through the cold winter months, was a picturesque farm with all the fences, painted white.

"When will I ever learn Heidi," the dog cocked her head to the right, ears perked forward as if she could actually understand his pain "All that liquor last night and Agnes is still dead." The cuckoo clock in the kitchen sounded off seven times, "Dang it girl, I guess I had better get over to Johns and do those chores. Christine will be waiting on me in town." Henry was not a church going man so usually there was no rush on Sunday morning to get anywhere. With Henry's demeanor, there really wasn't ever a rush to get anywhere. But, he did need to do a few chores at John's place and then gather up the clothes his neighbors would need for their stay in town. Henry thought about his friends the Kreutzer's as he made the short ride to their farm less than a mile from his.

John had been in America for a couple years. He had come over to run the farm when his Uncle Herman was killed in a threshing accident. John worked hard, had a couple of good crops and was able to purchase the farm from Aunt Matilda. John's wife Christine and the girls, Agnes and Grace, joined him here just last year. Henry unfolded the list of things Christine said they needed in town and placed it on the dresser top. Then, he laid a blanket across the bed and placed several shirts, trousers and a suit coat on the blanket. Next he laid out dresses, and finally rolled them all up, tied them with a couple belts and secured the roll behind his saddle. Putting some smaller items in his saddle bags, Henry finished his load by tying a hat box to his saddle horn. Departing for town, he should be at the hotel at least an hour and a half before church.

Liberty Township roads were fair as long as they were dry. They were improving but still made the trip a little longer if you were driving a wagon. Henry had his own shortcuts and Nina, Henry's Medicine Hat pinto, knew them all. The one through the buffalo wallow field was Henry's favorite. Today, it was appropriate that he take it. North Branch Creek was low now so crossing it was easy. Henry figured there must have been a beaver dam on this creek long ago, maybe even a thousand years. It must have been a site to see and he envied the Natives for having that opportunity. That beaver dam probably created a small lake, ten acres maybe. Huge buffalo herds would graze on the endless prairie grass, and drink from this lake. After bathing, they would roll in the dirt. Thousands, even millions of the beasts dusted themselves in these very wallows, creating these craters, some six, even seven feet deep!

Up and out of the wallows, the prairie flattened out for as far as the eye can see. The grain elevators in Parkston, those skyscrapers of the prairie, came into plain site even though the town is still two and a half miles away. Henry pulled gently on the reins and with a soft "whoa girl" stopped Nina, whose name in the native tongue means mighty, in front of the gate to the Dakota City Cemetery. Henry slid down from the eleven hand tall mare, looped the reins around the saddle horn and let the pony loose to graze on some wild alfalfa shoots. "This will be a sad place come tomorrow" Moss thought to himself. "I always liked this little cemetery, with Dakota City gone now, it will stay small." Henry tugged on the leather gloves he had tucked in the back pocket of his denim jeans, slipped them on, and then tossed his hat behind August Gertz's headstone. The prairie wind was beginning its daily howl and his hat would be safe there. "Russian thistles," Henry mumbled to himself as he tugged hard, pulling them from the earth. "I always wondered what God was thinking when He created these curses to our beautiful prairie. Cows won't eat them and they suck up what little moisture we get out here." Having cleared the weeds off the plot of ground, Henry stomped down hard in the dirt with his right boot heel and started backing up, marking the four foot by eight foot grave site for the grave diggers. "I told John and Christine they could have my plot here. There's plenty of room for all of them when they need it. Someday, I'll buy a single plot over there by those scrubby pines for me. Without a family, I don't need this much room anyhow." Just as Henry was turning to retrieve Nina, something odd happened; a crow landed on one of those scrubby pines. CAW...CAW. Henry was flabbergasted. It was as if that usually cautious crow was cawing to him. Then he figured it out. He remembered a Lakota scout he served with in the army had told him that the spirits will send a messenger to earth after the death of a loved one telling us that the soul of the departed has arrived in heaven. "Could this crow be that messenger? I'll be darned, Henry thought, she made it!"

The town of Parkston was a big square section, one mile by one mile, Henry rode in from the southeast and just at the edge of town slowed down to gander at that new warehouse being built. "So Wiseman's the one doing this huh, I never gave it much thought till now." It was a few minutes before nine o'clock when he passed the flour mill and the ball field, then coaxed Nina west on East Main Street, a dirt street about forty feet wide. The first business on the east side of Parkston was Everett's welding shop, right across the street from the sorghum mill that made some of the best syrup in the state. Houses lined either side of the next six blocks until he reached Railroad Street, or, grain elevator row. Across the tracks sat the depot on his right and a hatchery on his left. A gentle pat on the rump with a switch that doubled as a fly swatter sent his horse into a trot that quickly took him the last block to the front of the Saint Charles Hotel.

"I am up here Henry." It was John, hanging out of the window of a third floor room. "You got things for us?"

Henry held the hat box up and waved it around a little, "I'll be right up John." Main Street was pretty quiet this Sunday morning. Most people weren't in town yet for church services. Most services were late in the morning so farmers could get chores done. When all those Catholics and Protestants got in here, Henry figured it swelled the regular population of Parkston to close to a thousand. That's a lot of hot air on an already hot summer day. Henry liked the town; he just couldn't quite understand why these church goers didn't like each other. He finally just figured it must be some bad feelings they all brought over from the old country. John met Henry at the door, "Sorry you can't come in, the missus need this dress. Thanks for doing this for us."

"Shucks John, it isn't anything."

"Are you coming to the visitation this afternoon Henry? I know you don't really like churches but this is at the funeral parlor."

"Yea I'll be there, John. In the meantime, I need to find a shady spot to rest a little. We had a little wake of our own at Bennie's Place last night."

"You rest, Henry; I will see you this afternoon."

Except for an occasional squeak from a Philadelphia fan hanging from the ceiling in the gathering room, the funeral parlor was quiet. Only a few people were there to view the casket of young Agnes. Didn't make much difference, her casket was covered in a black shroud. Except for singing in the church choir and helping children in Sunday school, she had few friends. She did not attend school because her family needed her to work at the hotel.

"Agnes was the hardest working girl I had. She stood over that Columbia Rotary washing machine for hours and when she was done with my work, would take in laundry from guests to make some extra money!" Cliff and his wife, Carlotta, were visiting with John and Christine, Gracie was napping on the couch. Carlotta held Christine's hand as they spoke to each other in German. "You know what I always liked about Agnes? She was the happiest girl in Parkston. She would clean rooms and sing. She would help in the kitchen and sing. Her favorite job was hanging sheets out on the line, she loved getting outside, she could sing louder!" Carlotta gave Cliff a piercing glare, "It was a sad day when Clifford let her go to work in Sioux Falls." Cliff knew they were talking about him but because he didn't understand the German, he simply shrugged his shoulders.

Henry was standing by himself in front of a window that faced west toward the Catholic Church. "You mind if I join you Henry?" It was Father Mullaney. "The new church is quite impressive, you agree?"

"It is big, yes."

"I don't mean to pry; I have a very large congregation and am not desperate for members. But I am curious, and concerned for the souls of all people. Why is it you don't believe in God Henry?"

Henry studied Father's face, it was a young face, and he seemed genuinely concerned. "That is a fair question Father, but I do believe in God. My God just doesn't care if I go into a church or not."

"I don't understand why your God would not want you to build buildings to recognize how great He is, it is what we do."

"That is how your religion fits you Father. Now don't get me wrong, but if I wanted to go to one, how would I choose from all the churches in this town? Besides, none of you get along anyway. The way I see it, there was people all over the world long before Christ came along, are they all lost souls because they didn't know of Him? I commune with my God every day through nature. It is similar to the Natives and their Spirits. It is hard to lie down under the stars and not to think there is a God responsible for the world. Or, to ride your pony like the wind to find shelter from a prairie thunderstorm and not think there is a God responsible for it. The way I see it, God is good and bad. When I see children playing, I think God is good. When I see a dead child, Henry motions toward the casket with the hat in his hand, I think God is bad. Right now I am not happy with God." Henry paused for a moment and thought. "All I can do is to try and be a good man. I do not steal or covet my neighbor. I do not cheat in my business with others and I do not kill except to protect. I try to treat all creatures with respect. No disrespect Father, but there is no building man can build, no matter how large and rich, that can compare to my church!"

"Well said my friend, but if you ever feel that your life is out of control and you need help, remember the church is always open for prayer. In God's house, everyone can have a personal relationship with Him through Jesus Christ."

Cliff excused himself and went out the front door to have a smoke. Ben, Henry and John followed. John didn't smoke but the others cupped their hands against the wind and lit up. Father Mullaney walked out to the veranda and joined them. "I am so sorry for the few people that came to visit Agnes this afternoon, I urged the congregation to show support…"

"I know you did Father, and we thank you for that. I am sure it is because they think this mysterious disease that killed her is contagious. Lord knows we have had enough of those epidemics." John was sincere.

Cliff cheered things up as he usually did. "I have an announcement if anyone is interested. You are all invited to the hotel for supper tonight. Carlotta and I have prepared a small buffet for the family and friends. Some of our staff that worked with Agnes will be helping. It is in our private banquet room so there will be beer and," Cliff gave Father a wink, "wine available."

"Well, in that case I feel obliged to come! What time do the festivities begin?"

"Six O'clock, the bar is open!" Cliff pulled the rope that clanged the bell signaling the party had begun. It may seem strange to some that there would be a celebration at such a sad time, but with epidemics, strange diseases and horrifying accidents involving the crude machinery farmers used, death was common on the prairie. One out of five men shaking hands did so with one or two digits missing. Cliff started with a toast, "This is not a celebration of the death of a friend, but a celebration of her life! Ronnie, Andy, some music please, Agnes loved music!" Ronnie and Andy played the accordion and the guitar respectively, neither of them very well. But they could carry a tune and were always happy to do it. Besides, their music was a welcome diversion to the mundane rural life of the upper plains.

The accordion wheezed a little but was soon enough pumping out polka songs that got your foot tapping the floor. The banquet room at the hotel was large enough to seat a hundred people so there was plenty of room for Ronnie and Andy to move about the crowd. Clifford asked his good friend Ben if he could tend to the bar while he put the finishing touches on the meal. Guests passed the buffet to see if their certain favorite food was on it, most all of them were. There was a choice of fresh garden lettuce, cottage cheese, olives, carrots, cold sausage and cheese. The rest of the buffet consisted of sourdough bread, sweet butter, bratwurst, sauerkraut, cream corn, beans, mashed potatoes, gravy and then, fresh from the smokehouse, a prime roast beef, cooked to perfection in Carlotta's kitchen and sliced and served to you by Cliff. Needless to say, the dinner was enjoyed by all. After dinner, the men enjoyed a cigar and passed some stories.

"Dang John, I passed through those buffalo wallows this morning on my way into town, you been through before haven't you?" Henry was teasing his friend and put him on the spot.

John blushed, "Yes, Henry, I can't forget about the wallows because you keep reminding me!"

"What about the wallows? You two find something out there?" Ben was enjoying a cigar after the feast Walter Wiseman had paid for.

"The wallows are where I first met Agnes. You tell the story John, you were there first!" Zach and Father Mullaney pulled up a chair.

"It was Christmas Eve last and we were returning home from the church in town. It had been snowing and Christine was worried that we would not get home before it got dark." John felt hands on his shoulder, he knew those hands belonged to Christine. John cleared his throat and started again. "It was snowing hard, and I was worried that we would not get home before dark. The wind had not yet started up and I knew that when it did, we may not be able to see anything. I decided to go through the wallows."

"What, you can't get a wagon through there when it's dry let alone in a blizzard, what happened next?"

"Agnes and Grace, bundled up with blankets in the back of the wagon, were singing Christmas carols, Silent Night I remember…we had gone in about a hundred yards and it looked like it would flatten out some. The wind was blowing snow into drifts, but I was sure I had made the right decision. Then…a jack rabbit bolted from one of those drifts and ran right under the horses. They spooked, reared and spun hard to the left, snapping the hitch-pin like a tooth pick. The jolt sent Christine backwards over into the wagon with the girls and by the time I let go of the reins, me head first into a snow drift! I got up just in time to watch my family careen deep down into a crevice. My team disappeared into the storm. We were all right, but in a lot of trouble. It was still over a mile to the farm and the twenty minutes I thought I would save might now cost us our lives!"

Father Mullaney was beside himself, "What did you do to get out John? It is obvious you all survived!"

Christine, who could understand English much better than she could speak it, spoke slowly. "Fader, John got us in, but…he could not get us out! Henry Moss got us out. You tell them John." Henry didn't like to hear about himself much, but he was a little proud of this one.

"We had been stuck in the snow and mud for maybe fifteen minutes and it was getting darker. Christine and I looked it over and couldn't figure out what we could do. We could try to walk, but would probably get lost in the storm. We could stay in the wagon, which was tilted just a little to one side. It would give us protection from the horrible wind. We had blankets and decided we would stay. We just hoped the horses would find their way to the farm as we could not afford to lose them. Well, the horses did not make it to the farm, they came back to us. Agnes was the first one to see Henry leading the team in. You were happy you found us, Henry?"

"I sure was Johnny; I remember Agnes said something in German like I was her Knight in a shiny yellow slicker!" I'm just glad I saw those wagon tracks leading into the wallows. I knew I had to see who was crazy enough to go there with a blizzard bearing down!"

Zach asked. "How did you get the wagon out?"

Henry continued, "I had pulled a lot of wagons out of mud and snow in the army, and my horses always got the job done. It took all of us to get the wagon set up straight...Agnes and Gracie helped too. They of course thought this all a lot of fun. Then, we just backed the team down and used the rear hitch pin. Out it came! Everyone jumped up and down and celebrated. We got the Kreutzer's all loaded up and went to my farm, it was closer, made it by dark to, didn't we John!"

There were many more stories that evening. Some would make you smile, and some, like the story of how this family had lost two daughters in five years, could make you cry. It was a sad day, but a good day. A day when the Kreutzer family realized they belonged in Parkston, South Dakota.

Chapter 4

Monday June 4, 1906

"Ashes to ashes, dust to dust, we render the remains of Agnes Kreutzer, born October 3rd, 1889 and died, June 1st, 1906, back to the earth. May God have mercy on her soul and may she rest in peace. In the name of the Father, the Son, and the Holy Spirit, Amen." Just as Father Mullaney finished speaking, a gust of wind sent dust swirling around the mourners. Like a tiny cyclone, the voluminous burst sent hats flying across the prairie like tumbleweeds. The few friends and neighbors who had gathered at Dakota City cemetery retrieved them, climbed into their buggies and departed for town. Rothe and his helpers, Ray and Theophil, waited quietly in the background for everyone to leave before permanently covering the grave with virgin prairie sod.

Once again Henry chauffeured the Kreutzers the two miles back to town. John pulled his derby down hard on his head. "Thank you for being here Henry. Christine and I thought staying in town today would be good for us. We will go back to the farm tomorrow."

"Agnes wrote no letters, you think it…how you say…for her being sick?" Christine was melancholy, her motherly instincts telling her something was wrong.

"It is possible. You would think they would have let us know that she was sick. We could have gone to get her and bring her home." John was confused. He and many others had questions. But he had trusted the Wiseman's with their daughter. If the doctors in Sioux Falls said she had died suddenly of some unknown disease, who were they to say otherwise. John took Christine's hand and squeezed it gently. "God's will is done my dear, it is finished." Christine gazed up at him with her red, swollen eyes and nodded.

Back in Parkston, the few friends who had attended the graveside service gathered at Ben's Place to have some lunch. Ben, his wife Rebecca, and little Miss Madeline were joined by Cliff and his wife Carlotta. Floyd, a local barber, closed his shop across the street for the noon lunch hour and joined his friends.

"Papa; would the sickness that killed Agnes leave cuts on her head?" twelve year old Madeline asked.

"I don't know Madeline; no one has seen the body. Why would you ask such a question?"

"Well, I, I guess I kind of peaked in when Father was giving Agnes her last rights."

"Are you saying Father saw this too?" Cliff's interest peaked.

"Yes. It was Sunday morning before church. Mother went early for confession, and I wanted to pray for Agnes. I watched for Father, he went across the street to the funeral parlor so I followed him. He opened the casket and performed the blessing. He seemed to stare at Agnes as if something was wrong. When he turned away, I snuck a peak! I saw her real good Papa. She had big cuts on her head. They were real cuts Papa!"

"Father must have seen you."

"Yes, he was surprised that I was there. But I said I was sorry. He told me to keep it our little secret. Am I in trouble again?" Madeline asked. Ben paced, thinking, "Of course not honey, you were just being loyal to your friend...Karl?"

Karl Langerman, a young Parkston attorney and poker playing friend of Ben's had just sat down. "What can I do Ben?"

"You heard Madeline's story?"

"I heard."

"Go see if Father is at the church, he should be there. If not, find him. I'll go look for Doc Hughes."

While Karl headed over to the church to find Father, Ben went down the street to the doctor's office. If there was some kind of trouble brewing we would sure need Doc's opinion.

Ben wouldn't find Doc, Karl would! Doc Hughes was at the church at the begging of Father Mullaney. Father was describing the apparent cuts he observed on Agnes when he administered last rights. The atmosphere in the parish study was funereal when Karl rapped on the door. The two men waved him in and continued their discussion on a proper course of action. The men were acutely aware that they represented the three professions needed to make a big decision and did not take their responsibilities lightly. Medical, religious and legal aspects of an autopsy would all need to be considered. Was there sufficient evidence to justify an autopsy? What does the Catholic Church say about an autopsy? How hard would it be on the family? What if they perform an autopsy and they find foul play? Murder is a strong accusation, could they prove it.

The men reached a decision. The consensus is there is sufficient cause for an autopsy. The Catholic Doctrine is not opposed to obtaining the truth through an autopsy. Of course they would follow the wishes of the family. If the autopsy deems an investigation, we will be prepared to see it through! The next decision to be made was how to contact John and Christine Kreutzer for their permission. They called on Henry Moss. Doc, Father and Henry met Cliff at the hotel. It was late afternoon when Cliff went up to the third floor suite and knocked on the door.

"What could be the problem Clifford? Did we do something wrong?"

"No...no of course not, John, there's no easy way to say this. We have reason to believe that Agnes did not die from a disease and we have questions. Henry is downstairs with Father Mullaney and Doctor Hughes. Can they come up and talk to you and Christine?"

Puzzled, John responded, "Yes, yes of course, bring them up."

Cliff took Grace with him downstairs for a soda and the three men went up to confront the Kreutzer's with their stunning news, Henry spoke first. "We know you two have been through a lot these last few days but something has come up that smells pretty bad to us. It seems Father saw cuts and bruises on Agnes when he gave her final rights before burial. This is not an easy question to ask you John, we think we should disinter Agnes's body and perform an autopsy to see what may have happened."

"I ...we don't know what autopsy is."

Doctor Hughes explains. "An autopsy is like a surgery. We would simply look at her heart and lungs to see if there was a disease or if she had died from something else."

John, holding Christine's hand, left go of her and folded his hands as if to pray. "When our Sophie was a child, she and Agnes shared a small room in our house in the old country. At night, mother and I would watch and listen as Sophie taught Agnes how to pray. She would lie flat in bed; feet tucked close together under her blanket, and begin. Now I lay me down to sleep, I pray the Lord my soul to keep, if I should die before I wake, I pray the Lord my soul to take. Both of our girls are now dead. The thought of them asking the Lord to take their soul to Heaven is what we cling to. If you dig up Agnes's body and cut her open...will her soul be lost?"

The room was quiet for a few moments before Father Mullaney spoke in a soft voice. "My beloved Kreutzers, You have showed great strength lo these last few days and we ask still more from you. This autopsy will be hard but these men are good and have good intentions. In the eyes of the church it will do no harm to the body. We believe that at the time of death, God retrieves the soul and takes it back to Him. The autopsy will be performed on the physical remains. She will feel no pain or suffering. I am confident that He heard their prayers and the souls of Agnes and Sophie are in God's hands. They are now free of all worldly suffering."

John and Christine nodded in agreement, "May God's will be done, and you men have our permission."

Plans for the autopsy began immediately. Henry and the two men who buried Agnes, Theophil and Raymond Schulz, prepared the wagon and the tools they would need for their early morning dig. The plan would be a simple one. Henry and the boys would disinter the coffin, load it on the wagon, and let John drive the coffin the two miles to town. To avoid any small town gossip they would camouflage the casket with hay and grain sacks. Henry would meet John at the funeral parlor to help unload the coffin. The autopsy would be performed by Doc Hughes and assisted by Zachary Rothe, the local undertaker. They determined all of this would take all morning for sure so the Schulz boys would be back at the cemetery sometime after lunch to help inter the coffin.

Chapter 5

Tuesday June 5, 1906 dawned clear and warm and the doctor and his assistant were ready when the hearse pulled up to the rear door of the mortuary. It was seven am. The casket was removed from the wagon and placed on a gurney for the short ride up a ramp. Once inside, Father prayed asking God to bless the men and their task, and then took John across the street to the church. The gurney was then positioned beside the embalming table and the top of the coffin was pried open. Doctor Hughes had assisted in many autopsies in medical school at the University of Minnesota. He had not performed any since being named the Hutchinson County Coroner, a dubious honor seeing there were only four other doctors in the county, and one of those was a horse doctor. At least he had a seal to put on the file that would contain their findings. Rothe was not a pathologist, but was a licensed mortician and knew the human body. Each man had taken oaths to care for their patients and would show nothing but respect for Agnes.

"Now, Zachary, we will begin by just observing the general condition of the body. This should tell us a lot about what we are looking for. Karl has read the death certificate, signed by Sioux Falls physician Calvin Downing. Because the doctor listed the cause of death as diabetes mellitus and an unknown disease, Karl recommended we do a complete autopsy and study the condition of the internal organs. Feel free to talk about any thing you feel is relevant. Discussion is good and it would really help me if you would take the notes. Are you ready?"

"Ready." Zachary Roth was a quiet but confident man and Doc knew he would be a great help.

"Then let's get started. The mortician in Sioux Falls had dressed the corpse in a plain flannel garment. The casket was determined to be a closed one at that time, so no need for appropriate dress seemed necessary. The garment was removed, and with the naked body exposed before them, the men's immediate attention was drawn to the head and shoulders of the girl. Zachary recorded several cuts and bruises on the front and back of the shoulder area. These were made by a sharp instrument, perhaps a short bladed knife. There were what appeared to be 3 puncture type wounds in her back about 3-4 inches apart and quite deep. We will have to see if these punctured her lungs when we get her opened up. These puncture marks were unusual wounds and may have been caused by some kind of pick. Whatever caused them, they are quite recent.

"I never asked you, do you prefer to be called Zachary or Zach," Doc asked.

"Zach is fine."

"Then Zach it is, what do you think so far?"

"I am concerned about the cuts and bruises but I don't think they are the reason for her death. The wounds appear to be fairly fresh, there is no scar tissue. They are also clean, which would indicate the body was tended to at some point. What concerns me is this deep gouge on the back of her head. This could have caused the trauma. When we remove the brain we should look for hemorrhaging."

This guy knows what he is doing. "I agree with you. Now down here, this is pretty bad and would have caused severe pain. The skin has been peeled back from the leg and the nerve endings exposed, what would cause this?"

Zach had no answer and could only speculate; "burns would discolor the skin more wouldn't it? Perhaps it was caused by scalding, apparently repeatedly!"

Both men agreed that the general condition of the body was very poor with recorded notes listing fifteen different wounds that had broken the skin plus the poor condition of the legs. It was also recorded that Agnes had three broken bones in the fingers of her right hand. The collarbone on the right side was also broken and had actually punctured the skin. It was noted that this is the same side that the severe head wound was on. It is now time to open the body and search the inner organs for disease.

The body was opened using a y-shaped cut from shoulders to mid chest and down to the pubic region. Doc then made two incisions across the head, joining the bony prominences just below and behind the ears. The incisions are carried down to the rib cage and breastbone, and the cavity which contains the organs of the abdomen. The soft tissues in front of the chest are then reflected back. "You will need to cut the cartilages that join the ribs to the breastbone, use that small saw." Doc's concentration was intense.

The two men worked together very well and in less than an hour had gotten the skull cap and the chest cavity completely open with full access to all the organs needed. An inspection of the lungs showed no penetration from the puncture wounds on the back. The heart was the heart, in Doc's opinion, of a very healthy young girl.

"What is your opinion so far Zach, see anything out of the ordinary?"

"No, I have embalmed many a body Doc, except for external wounds; this girl should not be dead." Zach just shrugged his shoulders.

Doc held up a skull saw, "Let's get that brain out."

With the skull cap already removed, Doc very carefully cut free the attachments inside the skull. Once the brain was removed the two men measured where the outside wound was in relation to the brain. Hemorrhaging had occurred in the brain. Both men agreed that this could be the cause of death!

"I think we can start closing up the body," Doc said in a somber tone. I just hope what we found here this morning goes a long way in finding her killer."

"I agree," Zach said softly, "my only question is how this body got out of Sioux Falls without an autopsy?"

Doc Hughes and his assistant had hardly begun the autopsy when Henry Moss left the mortuary. He had felt awkward seeing Agnes dead. Henry needed some fresh air and a cup of coffee. Walking east up main street towards the Corner Café, he hadn't gone but a block when Karl Langerman met him on the bridge that crosses Pony Creek.

"How are things going up there Henry?"

"Ding-dang it Karl, we're trying to keep all of this quiet and you come meet me right in front of the newspaper house. You're the tallest man in the county and I'm the shortest, just walk slowly and maybe we can get to the café without anyone noticing us."

The two men marched eastward toward the cafe, the morning sun already hot on their faces. "I don't understand why you don't want Campbell to know what's going on Henry. He could be of some help."

"I do want his help Karl, but not yet. The way I see it, we don't know what happened to Agnes yet. The autopsy should help answer that. Then our job is to get the body back to the cemetery and buried properly. Campbell the newspaper man wouldn't be much help in that!"

Henry had figured right. Standing at the front window of the printing office was none other than Marion Campbell. Marion, a fine newspaper man, was a disciple of the great William Randolph Hearst. Campbell had actually met William's father, George Hearst, in the Black Hills of South Dakota back in 1880. George Hearst had owned controlling interest in the Homestake Gold Mine, the richest gold mine in the country. As a matter of fact, George wanted his young son William to manage the mine as a career. But, back home in San Francisco, The younger Hearst had only one dream. He wanted to run his daddy's newspaper, THE SAN FRANCISCO EXAMINER.

George Hearst was a realist who did not think his son up to the task. George asked his accountant, "How much will it cost me to let William run The Examiner?" The accountant said, "It would cost you

$100,000." George laughed, "Hell, that isn't any money." On March 4th, 1887, William Randolph Hearst became head man of the EXAMINER at age twenty-three.

The young Hearst was very energetic and wanted his newspaper to be exciting. Every day on every page he wanted to see words like violence, death, murder, suicide, sex and tragedy. Crime and violence is what sells newspapers he always preached.

Marion agreed, only problem was, Parkston didn't have any crime or violence!

"Frankie, what are you doing back there? Grab a cup of coffee and get up here, Quick!"

Franklin King, Marion's printer and star reporter was quick to respond.

"What's up Chief?" Frankie liked to call Marion that.

"Have you ever seen those two men even speak to each other before?"

Frankie stretched his head out the door. "Looks like Moss and Langerman. I don't think I have."

"There is something going on. This morning around seven I saw Moss's horse at the Catholic church." Marion scratched his unshaven chin.

"Maybe it was early confession on a bad horse deal" Frankie thought he was a funny guy.

"No, to my knowledge Henry doesn't belong to any church. There was something else. A wagon was sitting behind Rothe's Parlor. It had hay on it. Isn't that odd? Why don't you follow them and see if you can find out anything."

Henry and Karl had just ordered some coffee when Frankie finally tracked them down in the Corner Café. He got a booth right behind them and it was pretty obvious he was eaves-dropping.

"The way I see it Karl, well if you are going to be my lawyer in this law suit, you had better be good. I talked to Ben Miller about it and he recommended you. Those crazy Zollmann brothers I sold horses to a couple months ago say the horses just died and they want their money back." Henry was talking loud enough for most everyone to hear.

"I'll take your side on this one Henry. Let's go over to the office and draw up some papers." Karl and Henry left the café and crossed the street to the basement of the German Bank Building where Karl's office was. Frankie King headed back to his office to report to the chief.

Henry killed some time and when it was time to get John at the church, he took precautions and went south past Preen's Tin Shop, then he walked west past the livestock and lumber part of town. In case Frankie was watching, it would just look like he was doing some business down here. Henry passed the old Fullerton Lumber House and arrived back at the church about 11 am.

The timing was good. Doc had signaled that they were done and they could come and get the body loaded. John and Father Mullaney seemed at ease with everything so they crossed the street. I told the men about Frankie King and we all decided to move quickly. Eventually everyone would know what had happened, but they just wanted to get Agnes back to the cemetery before the news broke. John left through the alley and went straight south on Fourth Street. That would take him out of town unseen. Henry Moss rode east down main street. Just across Pony Creek, Henry pulled his horse up at the artesian well right in front of the Parkston Progress news office. While Nina drank volumes of cool artesian water, Henry lit a smoke and tipped his hat to Marion and Frankie, watching him from the front window of their make believe San Francisco Examiner Newspaper.

This sleepy little prairie town that didn't have any problems other than the Protestants and Catholics couldn't get along, was about to change. Unaware of their role in this change yet, Doc Hughes, Cliff, Karl and Henry pulled up a chair around a table in the back of Ben's saloon. Ben had just served up a lunch of home made wurst and bread smeared with lard. To wash it all down, a couple pitchers of cold lemonade made it around the table. The men were waiting for Hutchinson County States Attorney Anthony Taylor.

Karl didn't like the quiet. "You really think the girl was murdered Doc?"

"I think so. At least that is what the autopsy tells me. For the sake of not having to repeat myself, let's wait till Tony gets here. In the mean time, and I do not want to sound like an idiot, but what the hell do we do now!"

The men all laughed. Each one had been thinking about it, but didn't want to say it. Here sits a bar keeper, a hotel keeper, a small town lawyer, a doctor, and a horse trader. Not exactly a crack team of investigators. Or were they?

Ben pitched in first. "Where do we start? I mean Sioux Falls is a big city."

Cliff agreed. "You would think she had to have gone to a hospital? Do you think it possible some one there could have done something wrong?"

"Anything is possible, and I do think she was in a hospital. All of her wounds had been treated by some one who had training. Henry, you go to Sioux Falls quite often, what do you think happened?"

Ben had left to get more lemonade so Henry took advantage of that. "I know Ben is good friends with Walter Wiseman, but Wiseman has to be suspected of something doesn't he? Will we have a chance at getting the law involved over there?"

Karl was a little skeptical; "Tony Taylor, our DA is good, but, Sioux Falls has a lawyer on every street corner. That's why I got out of there. You guys have to remember that up till last year Sioux Falls was the divorce capital of the entire country! It was a boom for the city, bad for ethics. Yea, Tony is good, but he will need some help."

The mood quieted as Ben returned to the table and spoke, "Something has been bothering me about all of this. When Walter called me Friday night with the news about Agnes, he was so concerned about not opening the casket. He kept repeating the fact she died of a bad disease. Now, we find out all of this. He had to know something."

"That would be a conspiracy of one?" Doc asked.

Ben thought for a second. "It could be more than one. I'm sorry, where were we?"

"Trying to figure out ways to find out what happened." Cliff mumbled. "Can the newspapers help?"

"I don't like that. I know that times are changing, but army experience tells me that if you want to sneak up on some bad folks, you don't let them know you're coming ahead of time."

Doc Hughes went next. "These ideas are all good and I know Tony Taylor well. He is a dedicated man. He will do a good job for Agnes and her family. But I think he will need help in Sioux Falls."

"You could go Doc, you did the autopsy."

"No…I'm thinking more on the line of experience with people, like businessmen have. Sioux Falls is a big city, who in Parkston has connections there?"

Cliff jumps in……Of course, bankers. Let's get our bankers involved!"

"Shit Cliff, that's worse than the newspaper at this point. The rich aren't going to help us."

Henry jumped in,"How about Tommy Shaw?"

"Bully for you Henry. He's on the grain elevators board. He knows more people around the state than Walter does. Karl liked the choice. But his father in law is a banker."

"A good banker I'm sure. Ben, you got some one in mind?"

"I'm thinking Jacob Balas."

Doc liked the choice, so did Henry and Cliff. Karl hesitated. "He's a bit crude in his ways isn't he?"

The men all smiled. "We've known Jake longer than you Karl. He's probably the most honest man in the history of honest men. Hell, he was the first town Marshall Parkston had. You know Jake was a professional boxer at one time. He kept that railroad riffraff in line. If Jacob Balas gets involved, Ben thought a second…Jake will get results…one way or another!"

"He sure will." Anthony Taylor had found his way to the parley. "I'm sorry to be so late. The stage broke a wheel at Varney's Crossing and it took Dick awhile to get it fixed. Ben, Cliff, Karl...you all doing okay?" Hand shakes all around the table led to Doc. "Doc Hughes, the man of the hour, I am looking forward to seeing your report but, I don't believe I have had the pleasure of meeting this man."

"I am sorry Tony. This is Henry Moss, Henry, meet Anthony Taylor."

"The pleasure is mine Mr. Taylor. I've heard so much about you. We have been trying to come up with some ideas to help out. Or...whatever it is you want us to do. After all you are the boss, and you do have a busy schedule," Ben poked Henry, embarrassed, Henry just sat down and shut up.

Tony Taylor liked being the boss. He was a third term DA in a young and raucous county so it was evident the people of Hutchinson County liked him. Tall, tan and slender, he looked confident. "Tell me Doc, what did you find out this morning?"

Doc Hughes slid his notes across the table for Taylor to peruse. "The first thing we do in an autopsy is to just observe the general condition of the body. What struck us the most about the condition of Agnes Kreutzer's body was the absolutely hideous condition it was in! There were numerous cuts and bruises on her face, even burned skin on her legs. When you men return from Sioux Falls, one of the answers I want is how that body got out of there without an autopsy!"

Tuesday afternoon wound down into Tuesday evening and the pitchers of lemonade were replaced by pitchers of beer. There were more questions than answers, but the men did agree Tony would need help. Tommy Shaw and Jacob Balas were both summoned, and both appeared. They were in. One other man appeared, that was not summoned, Marion Campbell.

Ben brought more beers to the table. "A round from our friend at the bar" The men all looked up and waved to Marion. "He says he would like a minute of your time Tony, if you don't mind."

Tony always believed in turning a negative thing into a positive; "If you are guarding the hen house boys, you always want to know if there is a fox anywhere near. Besides, I hold an elected office and he owns a newspaper! Let's see what he wants. Come on over and join us Campbell. I think you know everyone here."

Marion was intimidating for a small man, maybe because of his intelligence. "Thank you for letting me join you. I don't know what you all are planning, but I wish you success in whatever it may be. I just wanted you to know Mr. Taylor, if there is anything I can do to help, please let me know."

"We appreciate that greatly Marion. Is it alright if I call you Marion?"

"All my friends do Tony." Marion wanted to be an ally.

"Marion, all we can tell you at this point is we think there was some mischief in the death of Agnes Kreutzer, you know her?"

"I wrote up a small obituary from the information Father Mullaney gave me, but no, I didn't really know her."

"I'm sure you know about the autopsy this morning. As a result of it, Tommy, Jake and I are leaving for Sioux Falls in the morning to see what we can find out. We would like to keep a lid on all of this if possible."

"Then my only line in Thursday's paper will in the locals. Maybe something like, three Hutchinson County men left for Sioux Falls on Wednesday to attend to some unfinished business!" The men smiled and raised a glass for a toast to luck in Sioux Falls.

"Two things I think you might want to know about Tony, part of my job in reporting news is to know what goes on in other cities as well as my own. News out of Sioux Falls is that there are three or four unsolved murder cases under investigation with little or no progress on any of them. The local police and the District Attorney over there, Leland Cobb, are under fire from the newspaper men. You may want to be careful not to piss off anyone. The other thing is the scuttlebutt on the streets in Parkston. Word out there is that Walter Wiseman may be incriminated in some way. Is that true?"

"Don't know that yet Marion, why?"

"Well, that new warehouse he's building out on the edge of town is giving four men full time jobs and putting money in cash registers all around town. Talk is Wiseman may even be the future of this town if he builds a brewery out here when the Indian Lands open up. That could employ twenty; even thirty men and jobs are scarce. All I'm saying is people in Parkston like Wiseman. You may not want to piss off to many people here either!"

Tony pulled Marion off to the side. "I see your point and thanks for the advice. The next few days will be very difficult on these men, but at the same time, so very important to the Kreutzer family, this town and the county. I am confident we are right. I learned this in law school my friend, Justice is like a greased pig, it is hard to catch, and even harder to hold on to!"

Chapter 6

Wednesday June 6, 1906

Henry Moss loved Lily Sullivan. He always suspected it, but didn't know what to do about it. She is so beautiful he thought. How could she be attracted to me? Strong and independent, she was sometimes intimidating, maybe to intimidating. Now, after Agnes death, it's been gnawing on him real bad. Henry mumbled some more to himself as he tossed the same feather light pony express saddle his daddy used nearly fifty years ago up on Morning Star's back. "What if Lily and I had not argued at Easter? What if I had gone over there to see Lily and the girls every couple of weeks like I had been doing the past two years? Yes, Henry Moss loved Lily Sullivan; it's been gnawing on him real bad.

Christine was weeding the garden on the shady side of the house when Henry reined his fleet-footed little gelding in. "Sorry for raising up all this dust, this pony senses a good ride coming on and I can hardly hold him back!"

"You go to Sioux Falls Henry?"

"I go to Sioux Falls Christine, but, first I need to talk to you."

Christine pointed toward the barn, "John and Gracie are there."

"If it's alright ma'am, I would like to talk to you alone before I go."

Apparently she didn't understand what Henry said. Christine slowly slipped two fingers from her right hand just into the sides of her mouth and let out a whistle that could be heard in town! John and Gracie came running out of the barn.

Christine giggled, "Agnes taught me."

They all went into the house and sitting around the kitchen table, Henry noticed. "You have five chairs around the table."

"Yes, we got one down from the attic for Sophie so we can remember what our family was like at one time. Sophie's death was bad, and now Agnes. It will help us get through all this and when the time comes, we will put two chairs back in the attic. What is it you want to talk to us about Henry?"

"Have you seen that pocket watch I gave Agnes at Christmas?"

"Oh no Henry, she took it to Sioux Falls. She loved that you gave it to her. We have not seen it and all her things are here."

Henry walked over to John and offered his hand as a friend. Then, inexplicably gave John a hug. Henry was weepy when Christine quietly asked what the matter was.

Henry gathered himself. "I think I am responsible for Agnes' death."

Stunned, they all just looked at each other, no one knowing what to say. John broke the silence. "But Henry, you loved Agnes like we did. How can you say such a thing?"

Henry was cautious. "Do you remember Lily Sullivan and her girls?"

Christine gave Johnny a little pat on the back. "Yah, yah we do Henry." Christine chattered away in German, so fast that Henry couldn't follow. John would translate. What Christine said was, "we had Christmas last at your house with them. It was wonderful. Let me see...Doris and ...Anna. Yes, Dory they called the oldest. Twelve years old I think she is. Anna is ten? Yes. Agnes, Gracie, Dory and Anna, they all capered around the house singing carols, and later we took that sleigh ride. You know you didn't fool Johnny and me. We knew you snuck those gifts under the tree. It was a Christmas to remember for all of us. It was our last Christmas with our beloved Agnes. But what do they have to do with this?"

Henry's mind, usually clear and focused, was cluttered with the events of the past few days, he spoke slowly. "I haven't seen or spoken to Lily for over two months."

John put his arm around Christine and asked her in German if she understood what Henry was saying, she did, and motioned with her hands for Henry to explain.

"I haven't figured it out yet. It all started last Easter. Lily and I took a buggy ride over to the Wiseman house to see Agnes. The mansion is on a large corner lot so we went past it several times to see if anyone might be around, there wasn't. We were about to leave when a man on horseback went up the alley way behind the house. We watched from the street and it appeared he was there to feed the animals. I walked up and asked him if he knew where Agnes was. He said no, but the Wisemans usually went to the Club on Sundays and sometimes took Agnes with them. The man's name was Nate Bumpers. He was in the employ of Walter Wiseman. We did not get to see Agnes, but we had the sense that everything was alright."

"What does that have to do with Lily?"

Henry sighed. "Lily looked so beautiful that day, red hair dancing in the spring breeze. I was looking forward to a nice evening with her when she suddenly said, pull over Henry, we need to talk!

John had pulled his chair closer. "What did she want to talk about?"

"She wants to quit the saloon business. Perhaps even leave Sioux Falls. Lily works sixteen hours a day and has no time for her girls who are growing up so fast."

"Where does she want to go?" John was curious.

"Anyplace I guess, Minnesota maybe, her mother lives there yet."

Christine asked the question. "What about you?"

"Lily asked if I had ever thought about leaving. Just going somewhere else and doing something different?"

Christine pulled her chair even closer, almost in Henry's face. "And what did you say?"

"I said I had never given it any thought and probably wouldn't."

"HENRY MOSS! It was lucky for Henry that Christine's tirade was in a part of the German language that Henry did not understand, John would translate. "Christine just wanted to know if a horse kicked you in the head when you were little. She also says, Lily asked you if you were thinking about her and the girls in your life and you say what? I never thought much about it! She didn't ask you to marry her. She was trying to see how you felt because you men, us men I guess, never say anything! Lily was probably worried you didn't like the fact she has two daughters, have you ever talked about that?" John was gesturing with his hands as if he was Christine.

"Ding-dang Christine, I didn't know you were that concerned about me." Henry was embarrassed. "Besides, what if I did ...you know, love her...and her girls, and they don't want me? You know a friend of mine who frequents Lily's saloon told me Dory and Anna do not like the men who hang around their mother, including me!"

Christine picked up her chair and slowly positioned it in front of Henry. She looked at John and said calmly, "I know you will tell him exactly what I say." She looked Henry straight in the eye and spoke, "poop on your friend. He speaks because he is jealous and could never have Lily. I watched Lily and the girls last Christmas. You did not notice because you are a man, I noticed, because I am a woman. The girls looked at each room in your lovely house. I know they were thinking that someday, somewhere, a house like this could be there home. Lily was not asking you for any kind of a long term commitment, she just wanted to know if there was any future for her family with you. Whether you love her or not Henry, you must talk to her. Let her know how you feel, good or bad, so she can get on with her life, and you with yours."

John relayed the message and had his own question. "Henry, how does all of this make you responsible for what happened to Agnes?"

"If I had not messed up with Lily, I would have been there for her. I could have gotten her out of there before this bad thing happened."

"We don't know what happened and until we do, you can't say you could have stopped it. Wait until those men from town return from Sioux Falls with some answers."

"I can't wait John, I stopped at the cemetery before coming over here and I made Agnes a promise. I promised her I would find out who killed her and why. Then I will know if I could have stopped it or not. Look, I have been alone all my life. When I was younger it didn't matter, I didn't want any responsibility anyways. Then I met Lily and things started changing for me. I didn't realize it at the time, but looking back, I just felt better about things, I worked harder and I felt stronger. I know I was wrong not to tell Lily about it, but I was afraid! I am no longer afraid. You Kreutzers have changed my life! You lose not one daughter to violence, but two! What do you do? You cling to each other even tighter. You pull little Gracie in and you go on with your life! I want that kind of strength, that kind of love, that kind of security. I want to lay my head on my pillow each and every night and pray to God thanking Him that if I would not wake up in the morning, that there was someone there to love me. To wrap their arms around me and mourn for me! You are right as rain Christine; I need to talk to Lily, for her sake as well as mine."

Henry grabbed his hat and ran out the door, in one motion he leaped up and over the horse's rear and landed right smack in the middle of the saddle. Then, as if he was taking out all his frustrations on this speedy little gelding, he gave his pony a spur. Together, they tore up the dirt driveway that led from the house to township road number five. The morning sun in the east was his target.

Henry's daddy was one of the original pony express riders out of St. Joseph, Missouri, 1859! Didn't mean much to most folks but it did to Henry Moss, he is a horseman. He makes his living selling horses. So, what he did was to develop a pony express of his own from Parkston to Sioux Falls! Each leg on the original express ran a horse hard for fifteen miles, station to station, remount, then fifteen more miles. Henry used the same concept. It was sixty miles from his farm to Sioux Falls. Four stations, or in this case farms! Henry employed four farms along his pony express route to board his horses. The ponies are on consignment to these farmers to sell. They feed and care for the animals and are free to use the animals whenever they need to. The only stipulation Moss puts on the farmers is that one of his horses must be available at all times. The first stop on Henry's express is Varney's crossing, on the east bluff of the James River. Glaciers cut the snake like route of The Big Jim millions of years ago. Each spring the snow melt from up north would dictate how much water would come through this valley. Most years, in the months of March and April, Henry couldn't get across here. But, by June, the river was depleted to but a small stream. Morning Star trotted through, his lead off leg of their journey a successful one.

"Morning Henry, You haven't been making this run in a couple months."

"No time to explain, Dick. Which one's the most rested?"

"Let me get that bay mare for you. Are you alright, you look different."

"I'm on a mission, a good friend died over there last week and it looks like trouble. They tried to dupe us Dick." Varney finished saddling the bay while Henry cooled off with a wet towel and filled his canteen with fresh water. "I know you'll take care of Morning Star, Dick, he's a good one, never should have gelded that one!"

"ALL ABOARD, last call for Parkston to Mitchell. Steam from the massive locomotive permeated the early morning air as the conductor cried out his boarding call. Didn't take but one call; Balas, Shaw and Taylor were ready. They shook hands in a gesture of good fortune and boarded. Only Gubby and Marion were there to see them off. That's fine for now they thought. If we do our job, there will many more people here someday to celebrate our success......or failure!

The eight AM train chugged north past Dimock, Ethan and then into Mitchell at a little past nine. A change to an east bound train was all that was required and it went smoothly. Each man bided his time in a different fashion. Jacob put his feet up and took a nap. Tony mulled over strategy, and Tommy Shaw gazed out the window of the train's lounge car. Not just one window, but up and down the aisle he paced to get a panoramic view of the land he loved. Blue, clear sky goes from here to what must certainly be eternity. Each click of the train passing over the connecting points of each rail mesmerized him. Click, click, hundreds of clicks, it helped Jacob nap. To Tommy, it was progress. This track was laid rail by rail. Just as the farms he was whizzing by were built one by one. The Homestead Act of 1865 was the government pointing the way west. A quarter of free land was yours for the taking if you could develop it. The civil war was over. The eastern states were filled up. Surely the settlers would flock into Dakota Territory. But no one came. The mystique of "the Great American Desert" may have held them back. Perhaps it was the Indian threat, Tommy didn't know. What he did know and was thankful for, were the Immigrants. They came by the thousands. They pushed, they prodded, and because of them, most of them succeeded. They broke this land sure as Henry Moss breaks a mustang. They were asked to do a job that no one else wanted to do. And then, when they succeeded, they were degraded and even despised by many so called Americans. Hell, except for the natives, we are all immigrants. I hope this country learns from this experience and never treats people this poorly again. Tommy was proud to be representing his immigrant friends in this pursuit. He would give more than his best to get justice in this case.

"Well I'll be..." Tommy scampered over to the starboard side of the lounge car.

"What Tommy, what's going on? Tony was up and looking around. Jake even woke up to see what all the excitement was.

The three men looked in amazement as a rider on horseback hell bent for leather raced up beside their Pullman car. "I'll be damned, it's Henry Moss! What the hell is he doing out there?"

"Apparently, Henry's on a mission. I hope it's the same one we are on."

"Don't worry boys," Tommy reassured them. "Henry was a horseman and a scout for the Seventh Cavalry. His experience will serve us well."

Henry gave the boys a yahoo and a wave of his hat and made his own entrance deep into the bowels of the Queen City.

Henry's first stop was at his old army buddies livery and blacksmithing business. ALEXANDER MCKENZIE LIVERY the sign read. Henry pulled up Coffee, the anchor horse of the four horse team, to a halt right under that sign. Alex, putting new spokes on a wagon wheel, tossed his tenoning tool aside and shuffled out to meet his old friend. "Henry Moss, you old son of a bitch, you can't leave a pony rode hard and put up wet, get old Coffee in here." The two sweaty men, one from a hard ride on a hundred degree day, and the other from pounding hot steel on a wagon wheel gave each other a hug. Actually, Alex gave Henry a bear hug. Henry, dwarfed by his six foot-five, three hundred pound friend just hung there in mid air with his boots dangling until the welcome was finished. "Good to see you Mossy, you want a beer?"

"Maybe one my friend, then, I have some business to attend to; you got a pony I could rent for a day while Coffee rests up?"

"Anything you want Mr. Moss, you saved my ass so many times in our army days, I'll do any thing you want."

"Is anyone renting that back room Alex? I could use a place to stay for a few days."

"It's available, but you know it smells like shit with all the ponies around here."

"Just like home partner...let's go down to the creek and cool off; I got a couple questions for you if you don't mind taking a break from work."

Alex laughed that raucous laugh of his. "Mind taking a break he says, I already put the closed sign on the front door!"

Alex and Henry plucked two bottles of beer out of the cold artesian water tank and walked down to a stand of cottonwoods that lined Dog Ear creek. "Reminds you of the Little Big Horn, don't it Alex?"

"You know it's been twenty years since we were there Mossy?"

"Yea, we dedicated that monument to Custer and his men that June day in 1886. You know it always struck me funny that the books all say no one survived the battle on that hillside. What about the five thousand Indians?"

"Your right my friend, this does remind me of that stand of trees on the bend of that river. Remember we strung our ponies along there and camped for a few days of festivities. It was eerie at night thinking about Reno and his men trapped up on that hill top on the other end of the battlefield. At night they had to send volunteers down through the Indian camps to get water. What a situation that had to be."

"Speaking of situations Mr. McKenzie, you remember when Colonel Hawke would come to us and say, "Boys, we got ourselves a situation, any volunteers?"

"Oh yea, I usually looked the other way, but not you Mossy, you liked those situations."

"I did, have not had one since we've been out, how long has it been Alex?"

"Ten, twelve years already I reckon. I figure you're here because of a situation?"

"I am. My neighbor back home, a sixteen year old girl, is dead. We buried her in Parkston on Monday."

"Well I'll be…what happened to her?"

Henry chose his words carefully so as not to upset McKenzie. Alex was a gentle man who didn't go looking for trouble, but for some reason he had always taken a liking to Henry and the trouble he got into was usually for demolishing some poor soul who gave Henry grief! "We think Alex, friends of mine in Parkston that is, that Agnes was murdered right here in Sioux Falls!" Alex hung his head and with his right hand made the sign of the cross mumbling for God to have mercy on her soul. "Alex, do you know Walter and Ruth Wiseman?"

"Yea, he's my biggest customer. I shoe all his horses at the brewery, why?"

"That is the situation. Agnes was a servant in his house when she was killed. We are here to try and find out what happened. Her death was real mysterious to us so after she had already been buried, we dug her body up and did an autopsy. It indicated some bad things. Someone over here went out of their way to try and cover it up, it might be Wiseman."

"You said we Henry, who is we?"

Henry smiled. "Let's just say of the Parkston men here to gather evidence; I wasn't picked to be with them!"

Alex just rolled his eyes and went to pluck two more beers.

Henry finished his beer and took his gear to his room. He didn't have much of a plan, just wanted to scout the area. It was about suppertime Wednesday afternoon when Henry visited what he perceived to be the scene of the crime, the Wiseman mansion on the corner of Sixth Street and Dakota. There was a small city park across from the house so Henry tied his pony to a hitching rail. It was a hot evening so there were a lot of people in the park escaping their hot houses. Henry just sat on a park bench and watched the house. After fifteen minutes and no signs of activity around the house, he walked across the street for a closer look.

"What cha looking for mister?"

"Ding-dang it boy, you scared the heck out of me. Who are you?" Henry was surprised by a ten year old lad.

"My name is Lester, what's yours?"

"Henry Moss."

"What are doing here Henry Moss?"

"I'm looking for clues Lester."

"What are clues?"

"Clues are something that will help me solve a crime."

"Well mister, if you think there is a crime here you need to go to that house right there!" Lester pointed to a two story brick house next to the Wiseman house. "The man that lives there knows everything, but be careful, he is real scary! The old guy is in a wheel chair." Lester ran away leaving Henry standing in the alley behind Walter and Ruth Wiseman's house.

A couple knocks on the back door of the house Lester pointed to didn't bring any results so Henry just sat back on his haunches and breathed in the evening air. "Look around Mossy!" Henry could hear his old army scout say. "See everything as it should be, then find what doesn't fit." Henry paused, looked left, right, up and down. Nothing; "that's ok mate, you don't usually get it right the first time out.

The back door was suddenly ripped open. "Did you knock on my door sonny? Most people of character go around to the front of the house!" Henry backed up a step, he didn't look down to many people, but this man, an impressive looking man who once was probably quite tall and quite handsome despite his evening stubble of whiskers, was indeed in a wheel chair. With the hot weather, the man's amputated legs were not covered with a blanket.

"Sorry, I guess I wasn't thinking. Lester said you might be able to help me. My name is Henry Moss, from Parkston." Henry thrust his hand forward.

"Yea, well Lester is a little tird. If I leave my shoes outside, he fills them with dirt. He thinks because I'm in a wheel chair I don't need clean shoes. Well, when I put my legs on, I need clean shoes. I don't like him. What else did he say about me?"

"Lester said if I wanted to find clues, I should see you. Lester said you know everything that goes on around here." Henry thought about what his old scout said about finding something different, this guy was different. "If you don't mind me asking, how did you get in that chair?"

"You cut right to the chase don't you boy. As long as you're here you might as well come in Henry Moss. Why you looking for clues?"

"I didn't catch your name Mister..."

"I didn't give it. Is it important to you?"

Henry was in no mood to banter. "No disrespect mister, but I'm not sure Lester is the tird around here. I got better things to do!" Henry walked to door.

"Like what? Spy on my neighbor? Settle down young fellow, stay awhile. I've been waiting for someone to start poking around over there. You're the first one I've seen."

"You see most everything around here Mister..."

"Sorenson, Vilas Sorenson. I was a railroad man for twenty years before the accident. You asked how I got in this chair, that's how."

"I am sorry you lost your legs."

"Don't be sorry. The Lord deals you a hand in life and you play it out. I just got dealt a shitty hand! I was trying to set a brake on a rainy day when I slipped and hit my head on the wheel, fell right down and the wheel took both legs clean off. Could have been worse, if it had been my head, I wouldn't be talking to you now!"

"Kind of like Agnes Kreutzer." Henry waited for a response.

"I don't know an Agnes Kreutzer, who is she?"

"A girl I know. She worked over there, now she's dead."

Henry studied Sorenson as he wheeled himself over to the window and gazed at the Wiseman house. There was a pair of Turner-Reich Prism binoculars on the window sill next to a half empty glass of whiskey. "Top of the line glasses Henry thought, don't know about the whiskey."

"First one I know of ever died. It's getting late Moss; I have to get ready for bed. You come by tomorrow morning sometime after eight, I'll be up here. I have an elevator but you can come in the back door and use the stairs. The door will be open, good evening to you!"

Chapter 7

Thursday June 7, 1906

With empire builders around every corner, a city full of power and cronyism beckoned the three men from the western prairie to call. Anthony Taylor thought hard about his future as he looked out his third story hotel room window. "It is a little intimidating thinking about who we would be up against this warm Thursday morning. Will I melt in front of these power laden men, or will I succeed and become one of them?" Jacob and Tommy were thinking more along the lines of where they were going to eat breakfast!

"Come on Tony, it's seven am and I need food if I'm going after whoever it is I'm after today." Jacob and Tommy apparently weren't intimidated.

The Grand Hotel was the place to stay in Sioux Falls. Located only a few blocks from the train depot and in close proximity to all of downtown, it gave the men a good base to work from. It also served the best breakfast buffet in town. The men ate as they finalized their plan for the day. Anthony gave his final thoughts as they finished the morning meal. "Tommy, you're off to see what kind of support you can get from the grain board right? And then to your father-in-laws bank?"

"That's right Tony. I'm thinking that's most of the day for me.

"Jacob, you say you know the sheriff. See what you can get there but remember what Marion Campbell said, we don't want to ruffle any feathers. You are on your own after that as we want you to get whatever information you can from whoever you can. I guess you could ask around about a lawyer. We should retain a local guy to help here when we're not here. The only name I've heard of is a guy named Kirby Johnson. I don't know much about him other than he represented an Olivet man once. Other than that, we're like a blank page; let's see what we can write on it when we get back here tonight."

"What about you Tony? What if the DA doesn't cooperate?" Tommy seemed a bit concerned about Tony's confidence.

"Leland Cobb is the real deal. He's been the Minnehaha County District Attorney for a lot of years so the people must like him. But, like Marion pointed out, the county has some murder investigations going and they don't seem to be getting any results. I'm thinking he may be a little vulnerable right now, ready to cooperate. Remember, the most important thing we have on our side is the element of surprise." Tony was animated, gesturing with his hands to make his point. "They don't know we are in town. They don't know what we know. What we want is contrary to their common thought. This will make them defensive to our common thought at first. We must break through their common thought and show them they are wrong. Then, we can lead them to our common thought!"

Tony Taylor sounded confident, but this was the first murder case he had ever worked on. Underneath the façade, Tony's guts were churning. Even though Minnehaha County District Attorney Leland Cobb's office was only two blocks from the hotel, Tony walked slow, thinking hard on his approach. Leland Cobb was one of the power brokers in town and Taylor knew it. One thing Tony did feel confident about was his appearance. Just under six feet tall and tan, he liked the way he looked. His long dark hair was lightly greased and combed straight back. Most men wore hats, Tony did not. Because of the heat, he wore an open collar, white, close-textured mohair shirt, fine and soft. One pocket, in style of course, accented the soft cuffs and pearl buttons down the front. A braided brown leather belt held up his mocha colored pleated cotton slacks. It was 9:28 AM when he stood before the attractive young receptionist for Leland Cobb. The girl raised her head from her Burnette Visible typewriter and her eyes met his. "Good morning sir, what can I do for you?" Her eyes perused Tony up and down. Taylor's did the same as the petite brunette stood and offered her hand. He gently took it and handed her one of his business cards, "I am Anthony Taylor, Hutchinson County States Attorney. Is Mr. Cobb available for an interview this morning?"

"No, I'm sorry Mister...the receptionist had to look at the card again, Mr. Taylor. Mr. Cobb is over at the courthouse this morning, I don't see your name on his schedule, and did you have an appointment?"

"Actually, I don't, and I am really quite embarrassed to just show up like this. I know how irritating it can be to just assume one can just walk right in, it happens to me all the time in Olivet." Tony was blowing a little smoke; Olivet was a town of around fifty people. It landed the Hutchinson County Courthouse because of its central location. "But it is important business, the matter arose yesterday and I traveled here just last night. Could you check his schedule and see if he has any openings?" Tony studied all the awards hanging on the walls as the receptionist checked the calendar. In one way he was a little relieved that Cobb was not there. Now that he had made the initial contact, the butterflies in his stomach had disappeared.

"Excuse me Mr. Taylor, I think Mr. Cobb may have a few minutes around 2:30 this afternoon but I can't guarantee it." With a cute little smile and a seductive shift of her hips to the right the girl added, "I will do my very best to convince him."

Tony was excited. Perhaps these big city folks won't be so hard to get along with after all. I do believe she is flirting with me. Tony returned the smile. "I'll be back this afternoon." Tony turned to leave the room but realized he didn't know the girl's name. He poked his head through the half open door, "I don't want to be rude, but if you don't mind, your name is..."

"I don't mind. It's Vera, Vera Cobb. Leland is my father." she smiled that cute little smile again and giggled.

"I'll excuse myself now." A pink blush colored his cheeks as he gently slid the door shut behind him. "I've done it now; she must be half my age. Yea, I'm a single man but gee whiz, the DA's daughter! Wait a minute, Vera Cobb...Cobb. She is single! I think I had better be early for my meeting with Cobb this afternoon."

Tommy Shaw marched in a different fashion parade than Tony. Western boots, denim jeans and a cotton shirt topped off with a straw cowboy hat was his attire for the day. Soft mohair or silk shirts cost $1.65, the cotton ones Shaw wore were 38 cents! His destination, the grain commission office, was on the sixth floor of the Grange Building. At twelve stories, the Grange, located at Third Street and Minnesota Ave, was the tallest building in the city. The office didn't open till 9 o'clock so Shaw took the elevator all the way to the top floor. He liked to climb to the top of his grain elevator back home and look out over the once wild frontier prairie that was now a patch work quilt design of farms and cultivated fields. From the roof of The Grange, he saw a different kind of history in the making. Looking east into the morning sun, Tommy gazed into the mist of the great Falls of the Big Sioux River. He thought of the native Indians meeting at these falls long before white men walked across them. From what he had read, when Columbus sailed the ocean blue in 1492, there were an estimated eighteen million natives on the North American continent. The 1900 census put that figure at somewhere around three hundred thousand. White man diseases killed millions of the natives as their bodies had no immunity to the invader's disease...for some reason Frederick Turner came to mind.

Frederick Jackson Turner, a history professor at the University of Wisconsin, had written several papers in the 1890's about the frontier being the central driving force behind American democracy. For most of the last three centuries free land to the West had been crucial to the American psyche. If a man failed at whatever he was doing, he could take advantage of free land to the west. No matter the natives were already on the land. The steady plodding westward by the white man would eventually eliminate that. Turner's theory went on to say, "now that the continent is filled up and there is no free land available, the frontier no longer exists. We must face the twentieth century realizing that democracy as we have known it no longer exists, just as the America we have known no longer exists." The 1890 census agreed. Although still in the minority, urban dwellers would soon outnumber the rural folk. Turner's writings were never really popularized, but were noticed and accepted by a few politicians in the East, most importantly, Teddy Roosevelt. Roosevelt accepted Turner's theory with vigor, and of course adapted it to his optimistic view of what twentieth century America should be like. If expansion was central to the health of democracy in America, Then it must continue. If the continent was full, then expansion must continue outside of the present boundaries of the country or democracy would begin to fail.

Shaw, an amateur historian of the plains, liked TR. What he liked most about the President was his progressive thinking. He worked hard to see that the little man had a chance. After all, isn't that what this investigation is all about? Protecting the rights of a poor immigrant against a rich opponent!

Tommy turned his eyes northward and focused on the perfect example of how big business could be brought down by the little man, cattle. Less than a mile from downtown stood the Sioux Falls stockyards. Always a symbol of the American West, cows came to define present day eastern South Dakota more than anything. Shaw had seen the great cattle ranches of the west. Feasting on the open range of the 1870's and early 80's, cattle barons had ruled the Dakota frontier.

But change on the frontier is inevitable. By the time the great blizzards in the winter of 1886 obliterated the large cattle herds, the change had already begun. Railroads had brought sodbusters and sodbusters brought barbed wire. The Homestead Act spelled doom to the big ranchers with the steady growth of the small family farmer.

"Good morning Mr. Shaw."

"Good morning to you, Jack Gross." Tommy knew the greeter without even turning around. Tommy was pretty convinced that smoking two packs of cigarettes a day for twenty years should put your vocal chords out of whack and in Jack's case, it had. "How have you been doing Jack?"

"I have been doing just fine. I got your note you'd be up here. I just had breakfast with my friend A. J. here. If I would have known you were in town, I would have invited you. You met A. J. Brash?" Jack asked.

"No, but I know of him. Well I assume it's the same A.J. Brash whose sign I see over by Dolton every time I ride the train to the city. A. J. Brass Polled Herefords, biggest Polled Hereford ranch east of the Missouri River. Glad to meet you Mr. Brass. Tommy Shaw, Parkston.

"The pleasure is mine Mr. Shaw." Andrew Johnson Brash was one of those big cattle ranchers who had made the transition to the modern cattle business. He raised registered Polled Hereford bulls and a lot of them. He even sells his bulls to Europe where they came from in the first place, heartier breed now.

"A. J. is the new president of the South Dakota Cattlemen's Association. His office is next to ours. Anyway, no meetings scheduled that I know of Tommy, what brings you to town?" Jack was curious.

"I don't ask for much Jack, you know that, but I have a predicament to deal with. It seems a young immigrant girl from Parkston was in the employ of your Walter Wiseman, She died a mysterious death in this city last Friday. Would you be interested in hearing about it?"

"Walter Wiseman?" Damn, of course we would!"

On the other side of town, Jacob was not having any success with the Minnehaha County Sheriff. Jacob did not lie when he said he knew the sheriff, he just failed to say the two didn't like each other. Jake was thinking that Sheriff Jimmy O'Rourke might know something about what was going on and that he would just screw up and tell him everything he knew. "O'Rourke, did you know a young girl from Parkston died in your town last Friday night?"

"I don't know that would be any of your business Jake Balas. Now get out of here, they shouldn't have let you in here in the first place."

"Why was a beaten up young girl's body let out of your jurisdiction without an autopsy?" Jacob had a short temper.

"You will have to go to the District Attorney to ask that. I only do what I am told." The sheriff did not budge.

"Look Jimmy, you know I'm not afraid of you or your high and mighty DA, we got a DA of our own. How you got to be sheriff is beyond me so you listen and you listen well. I am going to find out what happened to that girl and when I do, someone is going to pay! If you try to stop me, the same thing will happen to you that happened twenty years ago in Omaha when I kicked your ass in that boxing ring. You know damn well I'll do it too!" Balas stormed out thinking to himself, "that went pretty well."

Jacob was wound pretty tight after his confrontation with the sheriff. He needed to cool down and saw just the place to do that down the street from the courthouse, the Four Leaf Clover Bar. "Now that sounds lucky for me, I'll find that lawyer's office this afternoon."

"What will it be mate?" the bartender asked.

"Draft beer, cold if you have it." Jake spun his barstool around and looked the saloon over...nice. There were a couple of tables on either side of the front door. Large windows let the occupants at those tables watch the activity at the intersection of Main Street and Minnesota Ave. Good location; this must be one of the busiest intersections in town. The bar ran the length of the room with toilets at the rear. A dozen or so tables with green and white checkered tablecloths took up the rest of the lower floor of the building. The ceiling was vaulted upward to twenty feet or so with a second floor toward the back of the building. It appeared there was a meeting room up there, maybe an office. Jake couldn't see beyond the railing.

The bartender slid a foaming mug in front of Jake and asked if he wanted to order lunch.

"What?"

"Do you want to order lunch?" The bartender flipped a menu over to him.

"Sorry, first time I've been in here. I didn't know you served food." Jake was a little embarrassed, engrossed in the menu, he didn't notice the woman approaching.

"Do I know you? I make it a habit to know everyone who comes in to my place."

Startled, Jake spun his barstool around. "Whoa!" He was eye to eye with maybe the most beautiful woman he had ever seen. Five foot five inches tall with auburn hair, her low cut dress revealing cleavage Balas was having trouble keeping his eyes off of.

"No...no you don't know me. I am in town on some business and just saw your place." Jake's mind wandered, he was a married man, but not a dead one.

"I'm sorry. I didn't mean to startle you. My name is Lily Sullivan, the bank and I own this place. You are?"

"Jacob. Jake Balas."

"Where are you from Jacob Balas?"

"I'm from Parkston. It's a small town about sixty miles west of here."

This is interesting Lily thought. In the eight years she had owned this saloon only one other man from Parkston that she knew of had ever come in the place, and that man was the lover she hadn't seen in a couple months. "I bought a carriage horse once from a fellow from Parkston; I can't remember his name though. Silly, I just don't. Do you know anyone who sells horses out there?" Lily was teasing Jake.

"Yes, there are a couple of them. Henry Moss sells more than anyone" Jake said. "But he doesn't sell any carriage horses. His are mostly ponies."

"I know. I was dumb enough to by one. The first time I went for a carriage ride, the stupid horse took off cross country. Damn near killed me!" That got a good laugh from everyone and Jake felt right at home, Lily took the empty stool next to him.

"So you know Henry?" Jake asked.

"Yes. We've been friends for a couple years. He comes over here to buy horses every month or so. He stops in for a beer and lunch. I like him, have you seen him lately?"

"I have, he's here in Sioux Falls."

Lily felt a nervous excitement she hadn't felt in a couple of months. "Let me buy you a beer Jacob Balas, then you can tell me what's going on?"

"I guess I can tell you if you know Henry Moss and everything. This girl was a friend of Henry's. She was working in Sioux Falls for Walter Wiseman when she died. We are trying to find out what happened."

"JAKE, are you talking about Agnes!" Lily's heart sank. "What the hell happened?"

Henry knew he had a good lead in Sorenson; it was a little past eight A. M. when he tapped on the back door. "Vilas, it's Moss, you down here?" there was no answer, so Henry climbed the stairs to the second floor.

"I'm in here, down the hall on the left."

Henry slowly moved down the hallway, pausing to look at old pictures of Vilas hanging on the walls. Most had him with a woman in it, no children though. "Good morning Vilas, is it okay if I call you Vilas?"

"Whatever...you know, I've been thinking about this. You said the girls name was Kreutzer, long stretch from Moss. What's your stake in this?"

"The girl was a friend of mine. I feel responsible for her. Her parents are John and Christine Kreutzer, my neighbors out in Parkston. It's a small town about sixty miles west of here."

"I know where Parkston is Henry. I helped build that rail line back in 1886. We stayed there while we finished the line from Tripp up to Ethan. Parkston was way ahead of those other stops because that little town of Dakota City moved their homes and businesses there when the railroad missed them. Back then Parkston had a nice little hotel, a hardware store, a saloon, a printing office and even a post office. Is it still a small town Henry, or is it all grown up?"

"Grown up some, has about eight or nine hundred people I guess. You have a nice view of the Wiseman house from here, what are they like?"

"Don't know them much but things have changed over there. They used to be outside playing with their little girl all the time. That stopped a couple years ago when the girl died in a flu epidemic. Even money can't prevent a flu death I guess. Walter kept right on working...but his wife, she just got crazy!"

"How do you mean crazy?"

"She never came out of that house. She covered the windows with dark sheets to keep the light out. At night, with lights on in the house, I could see her roam around, walked through all the rooms as if she was looking for something."

"So you do watch the house at times?"

"I do, and I can say I've seen some things that might be of interest to you."

"So, you know what Agnes looked like?"

Vilas was silent for a moment, "The last girl I saw at the Wiseman house stood about five foot tall and weighed about, now remember Henry, I am describing her the first time I saw her some four months back. I would say she weighed at least one-hundred and forty pounds. I remember she was quite animated, lively for a portly girl is what I thought."

"That was Agnes alright. She loved to sing and dance about. When was the last time you saw her...I mean, it is summertime, I would guess she would be outside, right?"

"Wrong, I haven't seen her outside but a couple times in the last two weeks. The last time was, let me think, a week ago today. I remember because the same thing happened two evenings in a row. Wednesday evening just before dark, I saw her run from the house.

Well, run probably isn't the best word. She looked real bad, sick you know. She couldn't have weighed but a hundred pounds soaking wet. Ruth, Mrs. Wiseman, came to the door and hollered something in German. She looked real mad. I think the girl was trying to escape. I've seen Ruth chase other servant girls around the yard, one time with a butcher knife!" Vilas excitedly wheeled his chair across the room to the side window, pushing Henry out of his way. "It happened right down there by the well. The girl kept falling to the ground, like she was drunk. I'm sorry Henry, I don't mean to take this lightly, but it was quite funny. Ruth could no more stand on her own two feet than try and stop Agnes. They struggled for a bit and then Bumpers came out of the house to help. He just grabbed them both by an arm and took them back inside. Maybe twenty minutes later the house went dark."

Henry rubbed the stubble on his unshaven face. "Do you think Agnes was drunk?"

"I don't know, maybe. Could have been drugged, there are plenty of new drugs out there, like heroine. The world is going to hell in a hurry, although I wish I would have had some when this happened," Vilas picked up his stumps for legs and let them flop back hard against his wheelchair, "pain damn near killed me."

"What about the second time, you mentioned two different nights."

"The second night was worse; it was last Thursday about the same time as the night before. I wheeled over to the window and saw Agnes lying on the ground, apparently she had fallen trying to run. She looked real bad Henry. Ruth didn't come out of the house this time. She just stood at the door cursing the girl with words I never heard before. Agnes must have been real scared because she got to her feet and tried to run to the tack room. Bumpers came out to get her."

"Bumpers, Nate Bumpers?"

"Yes, you know him Henry?"

"Sort of, I met him over there at Easter when I came by to see if Agnes was at home, she wasn't. He said he was just doing the chores and that the Wisemans probably took Agnes to dinner, someplace nice is the way he put it. He also said that he was not allowed inside the house, how could he have come out of the house?"

"What a bunch of bullshit Henry! The Wisemans never took the girl anywhere. I would bet she was locked up in there. And, Bumpers is in the house all the time when Walter is out of town. You know Walter travels a lot. Anyway in the winter months, usually every other day, Bumpers hauls a wagon load of coal around to the coal shoot, shovels it down, then goes down the shoot into the basement. Funny, he always comes out the back door an hour or so later. I think to myself, Ruth Wiseman sure uses a lot of coal!"

"What do you know about Bumpers?"

"He likes to talk, mostly about himself. According to him, he and old TR won that Cuba war back in 1898 all by themselves. He says he was in Roosevelt's navy...a medical ship I think he said."

Henry returned to the window facing the suspect's house. "What did Bumpers do when he came after Agnes?"

"I don't know, I can't see the tack room from here, only the main house. The next thing I saw was Bumpers marching Agnes back to the house with a pitchfork stuck to her back. He was prodding her with it Henry!" Vilas hung his head in disgust. "If I had my legs I would have went down there and helped the poor girl. I am just a hopeless old cripple who let a young girl die."

"Don't be so hard on yourself. We all had a hand in letting this happen. Has there been anyone around the house? I've been watching but haven't seen anyone."

"Nope, they packed up some bags last Sunday and left. I haven't seen anyone come by but Bumpers since then."

"When does he do his chores?"

"Usually not till later in the day. Are you going down there Henry? I'd go with you if I could."

Moss didn't know what he was looking for but he went anyway. The tack room was open so he took a look in there. "Vilas said he saw Bumpers poking Agnes with a pitchfork. I wonder if I could get lucky and find..."

"Hey, Mr. Wiseman, I got a package from the Drug Emporium for you." It was a delivery boy with a brown box. "You want me to take it to the house?"

"No, I'll take it. How much do I owe you?" Henry paid the boy for the package and put it in a canvas bag hanging on the side of his saddle. He could check the contents of the bag when he got back to his room. Moss was getting a bad feeling about being here and resisted the urge to go back to the tack room...good decision, a rider was coming up the alley.

Nate Bumpers came off his pony in a hurry. "You must be looking for trouble mister. What you doing here?"

The last time Henry saw Bumpers at Easter, it was colder. He looked bigger with a coat on. Now, dressed for the summer heat, the man looked thin. Despite an unattractive shaven head and protruding eyes, Bumpers was still haughty so Moss took the offensive. "I guess I'm in the wrong place at the wrong time, Nate. Henry Moss is the name; we met last April at Easter time." Henry held out his hand in a gesture of peace, Bumpers didn't take it. "I was looking up my friend Agnes."

Bumpers backed off some. "I remember you...Agnes isn't here. She's gone away!"

Henry studied Bumpers and in the morning sunlight noticed something he needed to get a closer look at. Not wanting to spook the lad, he spoke slowly. "I know Agnes is dead, that is why I am here. Did she leave anything behind, personal things I could take back to her folks?"

"I wouldn't know about that Moss, I am not allowed in the house. The only time I saw Agnes was when she was outside sweeping the porch." He was apparently getting nervous with the questions and sensed trouble.

Henry pressed on, "I forgot my watch this morning, do you know what time it is?"

Bumpers, dressed in a dirty short-sleeved cotton shirt and a leather vest, pulled on the chain of his pocket watch. Flipping the lid open, he slowly studied the big hand, little hand, and then proudly proclaimed, "It's ten o'clock."

"Nice watch, can I see it?"

"I guess."

Nate handed Moss the watch and Henry took a good look at it. "Alaska Gold with a Swiss mechanism, fine watch Bumpers, where did you get it?"

"In the army, listen, I got a lot of work to do, can I have my watch back?"

Henry tossed it to him, "Look Bumpers, I am truly sorry if I caused you any concern by being here...oh; by the way, I was talking to your neighbor Vilas Sorenson. He was under the assumption that you were in the Navy, a medical ship he thought. I guess old Vilas must be wrong!" Henry calmly backed away to his pony. He knew he had better leave before he did something he would regret. The inscription on the back of the watch he had just tossed back to Nate Bumpers read, US CAV THE SEVENTH, and HWM. Henry Weaver Moss, it was the same watch he had given Agnes at Christmas!

Henry hoped Bumpers had got his cryptic message that the hunt was on and everyone is a suspect. Wrapping the reins to a hitching post at the park across the street from the Wiseman house, Henry anxiously placed the box he had purchased earlier on his lap. His razor sharp pocket knife easily sliced the box open. Henry didn't know it yet, but this would be like his Christmas present in June. He quickly took inventory, one pint of Vin Vitae energy stimulant, a tin of Dr. Hammond's nerve and brain pills and a small bottle of Dr. Hammonds Catarrh Cure All. Next, a contraption he hadn't ever seen before and a jar of some cream. Henry dug a little deeper in the big box and pulled out a smaller box, he opened it. Wrapped in cut up newspaper were two glass tubes; one morphine, the other heroine. There were also two syringes. My God, Henry thought, could Agnes have been on dope?"

The bell in the tower of the Episcopal Church several blocks west of Leland Cobb's office chimed twice. 2 o'clock. Tony gave a little wave to Vera Cobb as he closed the door behind him. "You are early Mr. Taylor. That is certainly admirable."

"Yes, I am early, I hope you don't mind." Tony had no excuse for being early except that he wanted to sit and watch the girl. Vera was very easy on the eyes.

"No, that's fine. Good actually. Mr. Cobb is in his office and has agreed to give you a few minutes." Vera had actually persuaded daddy to let Tony in.

"I appreciate that. Look, I am going to be in town for a couple of days and I was wondering…"

"Vera, send in my next appointment will you please." Vera, disappointed that Tony was interrupted, obliged.

Taking a seat in front of the head lawyer in this county, Tony thought to himself, "Vera's mother must be a beautiful; she sure didn't get her looks from this gruff man."

"I don't appreciate unscheduled visits. If it wasn't for Vera, you wouldn't be here. What is so urgent Taylor?" Cobb was a direct man.

"I appreciate you seeing me on such short notice Mr. Cobb. A matter I believe originated in your jurisdiction has me concerned. It involves a young girl who was working for a family in your town and now she is dead." Tony had delivered the first pitch.

"What girl, what family?" Cobb seemed rather disinterested as he reclined in his leather chair.

"Her name was Agnes Kreutzer. She worked for Walter Wiseman as a house maid to his wife. Her body was shipped from your city to Parkston last Saturday." Tony would have loved a glass of water to help calm his nerves.

Cobb sat up in his chair and glared at Taylor. "What kind of evidence do you have and where in the hell is Parkston?" Tony handed him the envelope containing the autopsy results.

"Hutchinson County, Parkston is in Hutchinson County and I am the States Attorney there." Cobb ignored him as he read the document.

"I thought you might want something cool to drink. Leland, Mr. Taylor?" Vera had temporarily saved Tony from the impending wrath of Leland Cobb.

"Yes, thank you. Water would be fine for me." Tony watched Mr. Cobb out of his left eye as he gulped some water.

Cobb stood up; he was much taller than Tony thought he would be. "Who performed this autopsy?"

"Doctor Hughes, a local doctor in town." Tony was getting more nervous as Mr. Cobb circled him. Thankfully, he had his water as a diversion.

"This Hughes, he is the medical examiner in your Hutchinson County?" Cobb appeared to be about seven foot tall as Taylor looked up at him.

"Yes. He is a good doctor. We have all the confidence in him. We think the findings justify an investigation and you are the man who can do it!" Tony sat up a bit in his chair in anticipation.

"Let me tell you how it works around here mister. You don't waltz in here with a piece of paper accusing a friend of mine of murder, and expect me to do something about it." Cobb was getting a little red around the temples.

"They are observations." Tony mumbled.

"What did you say?"

"I said they are observations, not accusations. I am simply asking that you consider the possibility that..."

"That's it, you are done. Time is up! If you ever come up with some credible evidence instead of these accusations, you let me know. And make an appointment!"

"I will do that Cobb!" Tony left the room thinking no nice guy any more, the gloves are coming off.

Tony did stop by Vera's desk on the way out and thank her for the water break. It had kind of saved his ass. And as far as his proposal to Vera to see her again...just say Tony left the District Attorney's office with a no from one Cobb, and a maybe from the other!

Tommy Shaw was having a great Thursday. He finished his meeting at the grain office and headed to the First Sioux Falls Bank. His father-in-law, President of the bank, Oliver Stanton, was waiting for him there.

"Tommy, have I got a lunch planned for you! It's on me this time. I know you joke about how I stick you with the check all the time, but everyone knows grain people have more money than bankers!" Oliver was obviously in a good mood.

"Why are you so excited about lunch?" Tommy was a little curious.

"We are going to have lunch at the most exclusive club in the state, the brand new County Golf and Country Club! Its a couple miles out there so we better get started." The two men caught up on news about each other and in about twenty minutes had arrived at the entrance to the club.

"So this is a golf course, how many acres?"

"We bought the whole quarter, one hundred and sixty acres. We are negotiating to buy more land for the future." Ollie was excited to show off big city progress to his brother-in-law. Tommy was doing calculations in his head.

"I figure you could raise about two thousand dollars worth of grain a year on this land, is golf worth it?"

"You farmers never quit do you? But you're right, it is a silly game. It is so difficult, it's almost embarrassing! I'm afraid golf will never be very popular, but look at this clubhouse!" Tommy couldn't believe his eyes. The two story brick clubhouse overlooking the nine hole golf course was the most elegant building Shaw had ever seen.

"Quite a sight isn't it? Most of us come out here because if you are any one in Sioux Falls, you had better be here. Money and power," Oliver took a deep breath, and then exhaled, "Let's get inside, I'm hungry."

Once seated, Ollie looked around the room to see who was here; he loved to brag about the company he kept. "Tommy, you see those two men sitting by the window?"

"Yes, I see them." Tommy was a bit embarrassed sitting with denim jeans, a cotton shirt and a jacket the maitre d' had given him to wear. "I wish you would have told me we were coming here Ollie, what about the two men?"

"The one on the left is Peter Olson. He is a shareholder in my bank, and more importantly, a doctor at the Methodist Hospital. The other man is Sigurd Paulson. Sig graduated from Johns Hopkins' University in the very first class of doctors specializing in forensic science back in 1889. He is the chairman of our State Board of Medical Examiners. Do you think they could help?" Stanton winked.

"Well you old coot! You had all this planned didn't you? Do you think you could arrange a meeting on such short notice?"

"I'll go talk to them, Tommy." Oliver returned after a brief chat with the two doctors. "He is interested but doesn't have time right now. But, they will be back here tomorrow for lunch if it works for you. What do you think Tommy?"

"We'll make it work partner, you may have just gotten us the break we need."

Jacob looked up at the clock on the wall of the FOUR LEAF CLOVER SALOON, 2 PM. Lily and Jacob had taken one of the tables by the front window and were just finishing a lunch of corned beef and fried potato slices. Lily spoke, "Can I ask you a question Jake? When you and your friends go back to Parkston, who do you have to help out here?"

"Tony says we will retain a local lawyer. Why, what are you thinking about?"

"You see that guy sitting over there by the window?" Lily hesitated, "he used to be a Pinkerton man."

"You're kidding." Jake studied him. "He doesn't look like a Pinkerton man."

"His name is Ivan Bausch. He used to be sheriff here years ago." Lily chuckled. "You have to excuse me, I've heard the story so many times from Ivan, I sound like him. "It goes back to when this was a dry state. Apparently a few of the richly-riches thought that prohibition didn't apply to them. They were mostly doctors, lawyers, judges and big business people. Well, Sheriff Bausch got tired of there debauchery and busted them."

"Well bully for him!"

"No, not really, the cronies targeted him for defeat in the next election and he was beaten badly, not only as sheriff, but as a man. The cronies planted false documents that accused Ivan of fraud and racketeering. Bausch never had a chance. His wife even left him. Ivan started drinking, hasn't stopped." Lily felt pretty bad for Ivan.

"Who were the cronies that got him?" Jake was watching Ivan as Lily told the story.

"The leader of the pack was, and still is, Walter Wiseman!"

"I think I'll have a talk with Ivan. Thanks for all your help Lily. I'm going to bring the boys around tonight to meet you." Jake was getting up to go over to Ivan's table when he paused, "by the way, next time I see Henry Moss; I'm going to tell him he's a damn fool. If I were him, I'd be over here more than once a month!"

Lily was excited at the thought of Henry being in town. It made her proud to see a loyal and caring side of him she hadn't seen before. But, she didn't get her hopes up to much or she'd be let down again. After all, Henry Moss had just about everything he needed on that pretty little ranch out on the prairie. Huh, nice to dream though!

Chapter 8

Thursday Evening, June 7, 1906

The three Parkston men met at the Grand Hotel Lounge to discuss day one of their mission. Tommy Shaw, excited about his success opened the meeting, "How did you do Tony, I was a little nervous about you this morning?"

Tony was a little melancholy for failing with DA Cobb "It went about like I thought it would, except that yea, I was more nervous than I figured I would be. It didn't help that Cobb has the prettiest secretary I ever saw. She flirted with me, too. Imagine, 33 years old and I can still turn a pretty girl's head. So I start to flirt back you know, old Cobb was at the courthouse. Where was I…yea, so I start to find out more about her…it turns out she is the great Leland Cobb's daughter?"

"Not!" Jake laughed that huge laugh he had. It was like it came from way down in him and resonated all around. "What did you do?"

"Well, what any district attorney from any rural county would do, I got the hell out of there! I did get to see Cobb though. Vera fixed it. He blew me off like a Dakota prairie twister. He says we don't have any credibility. I'll keep after him, her too. I know we can work on the same team. How about you Jake, apparently you stayed out trouble."

"Yes I did. You know, when I told you guys I knew the sheriff, it was the truth. I just didn't tell you we don't like each other." Jake waited for a reaction. Neither of the boys looked upset. "See, some people back home knew I used to do a little boxing. Actually, I made a living at for awhile on the Nebraska and Iowa circuit. Anyway, it seems one of the other boxers was the sheriff. Now, I'm not bragging, professionals learn not to do that, but seeing as that was about twenty years ago what the hay. When Sheriff Jimmy O'Rourke said to get lost, I simply told him to stay out of my way or I would kick his ass like I used to. How did you do Shaw?"

"Pretty good Jacob. I think its good news. First, I met with the President of the South Dakota Grain Association Board. What I did, and I hope it was the right thing to do, was set up kind of a back up plan for us. It worked out that the new chairman of the Cattlemen's Association was there so he sat in too. We discussed our predicament and they agreed to help in any way they could if we can come up with the proof we need. We decided that if we need them, they would put out a call to every member of their association. These members would carry our message to their local newspapers and in a matter of a few days we can have the word out all around the state. The consensus was that the majority of small towns would back us against the big city."

After a short potty break the three returned to the lounge to continue the meeting. Tommy started where he had left off. "I met my father-in-law for lunch, you ever met Oliver Stanton? No? Well, you will tomorrow. I took the liberty to set up a lunch date with Ollie and, now hold on to your beer, two local doctors. One, Dr. Paulsen, is on the State Board of Medical Examiners. They want to hear our case!"

"Bully for you Tommy Shaw! You may have just gotten what we needed. Tell us, where are we going for this lunch?"

"The same place Ollie and I went today. Have you heard of The County Golf and Country Club?" None of the men had. "It's new and it is fancy. They gave me a jacket to wear over my shirt. I was embarrassed. Anyway, this Olson is a shareholder in Oliver's bank and they both are charter members of this elite club. Ollie went over to visit him, told him why we were in town, and asked him the same question we have been asking ourselves. How did Agnes's body get out of Sioux Falls without an autopsy?"

"Apparently that got there attention, lunch is at noon tomorrow, but what about tonight? I for one would like some home town cooking!"

Jake was ready. "Follow me boys, I found a place today you'll like, and it's only a couple of blocks from here."

Jake, Tommy and Tony slid some chairs up to an empty table by the front window. They were lucky to get it. "It certainly wasn't this busy for lunch today. Wait till you see who owns this place. I'll bet she's around here somewhere. Yea, there she is, up there. Tony, you see her? She's the red-head talking to a couple of guys on the balcony." Lily saw the boys come in and waved at Jake.

"I know that smell, there is chislic cooking back there isn't there?" Apparently Tommy would order supper. "I'll go get a couple plates, just order me a beer."

While they waited for their food, Jake told Tony about Ivan, "I think he would be the ideal man for our team. He wants to help bring down Wiseman any way he can. There is the drinking problem, but Lily thinks if we show confidence in him, he'll stop." Tommy returned with fried potatoes and chislic piled high on a couple of plates. Lily followed him with a pitcher of beer and three shots of whiskey.

"I hope you enjoy my food, nothing but the best for my customers. I get the mutton fresh from a local farmer. He delivers the animals to that locker across the street. The butcher cuts the mutton into small pieces and slides the meat onto skewers. He delivers it fresh every morning, usually about seventy-five dozen a day! Are you going to introduce me to your friends Jake?"

"Sorry Lily." The men all stood up to shake her hand as Jake introduced them.

"Now sit boys. You mind if I join you?"

"Please, be our guest. Lily, have you seen Ivan? He was supposed to meet us here."

"He's here Jake. He asked me if I would stall you for awhile so he could try and relax." Lily rolled her eyes.

"Is he drunk?" Jake was surprised.

"No. He's quite sober. He just said being that sober makes him nervous! Here he comes now. Take it easy on him."

For some reason Jake had confidence in this man. Maybe just for the fact he had been a Pinkerton man. Maybe because he had been screwed over by the people we think had something to do with Agnes's death. "Ivan, I'm glad you showed up. This is Tony Taylor, the DA I told you about. This is Tommy Shaw, our great connection to the Sioux Falls hierarchy. You hungry? Apparently Tommy here thinks the three of us can eat two or three sheep at one sitting."

"No, thank you though. I am weaning myself from the bottle so to speak. The appetite may return soon, I hope. Jake has told you about my drinking?"

"He has, and we are with you on it Ivan. If Lily and Jake think you can help us, then I think you can help us. You agree Tommy?" Shaw had some doubts, but at this point, he figured they didn't have a lot of choice. Tony continued. "What we would like you to do is to keep an eye on the Wiseman house. Now, I understand there is some bad blood between you and the Wiseman's. Is that going to be any problem?"

"I would doubt if Walter Wiseman could recognize me from any of the other poor slobs he has buried in the last twenty years. No. It will not be a problem."

"Good, that is what I wanted to hear. We have a big meeting tomorrow and if things go the way we hope they will, there may be a lot of activity around the Wiseman house this week end. We will have to return to Parkston so we need you to watch the people who come and go. If you know them, make a note. If you don't know them, find out who they are and why they were there. And most importantly, if you need a drink, don't come here. Lily knew Agnes and would be very pissed if she saw you shirking. We need answers and think a Pinkerton man can help find them!"

Jacob had pushed his chair back from the table and was sitting up all proud of his accomplishment when Lily tapped him on the shoulder. She leaned over and whispered in his ear. Jacob breathed in her sweet smell. "I just wanted to remind you Jacob, you said the next time you saw Henry Moss you would tell him he was a fool for only seeing me every month or so, remember?"

Jacob was really enjoying this attention he was getting. "I remember Lily, and I will tell him."

"Then go tell him Jake so I don't have to. Henry's standing over there at the bar!"

"Henry Moss, get over here and join the party. I told Lily next time I saw you, I would tell you that you are a fool for only seeing her once in a while. There, I told you"

"You sure did Jake, me and about fifty other people. Thanks a lot!" The two men shook hands and Henry pulled up a chair next to Lily. She felt good about having her man back at her side. She was intimidated at times by his money and stature in Hutchinson County, but here, close beside her, he was simply Henry Moss, the man she loved.

A few minutes after everyone had settled in around the table, Tony, who was seated across from Henry and Lily, asked Henry what he had been working on. "I have been trying to piece together the events leading up to her death. A neighbor of Wiseman's been helping me, his name is Vilas Sorenson. I have also talked to Nate Bumpers at the Wiseman house."

"You were at their house?"

"Yea, I even bought a box off a delivery boy that was meant for the Wisemans." Henry walked over and got the box from the bartender who was keeping the evidence for him. He placed it on the table and everyone pulled up to get a closer look. Henry slid his arm around Lily as she pressed her body close to his. It felt good to have her back at his side. "A delivery boy thought I was Wiseman so I just paid him for it. I didn't steal it."

Lily playfully poked Henry, "Come on Henry, open it."

"Well, I don't know what all of it is, but there is some Vin Vitae, and some Dr. Hammonds nerve and brain pills." Henry was passing the contents around as he emptied the box. "I don't know what this is, but it comes with instructions." Henry held up this rubber cup on the end of a six inch stick. The cup was about four inches in diameter and was actually quite heavy. "It comes with this jar of cream called Princess Bust Cream...Oh!"

Lily was tugging on Henry's arm trying to stop him, she whispered in his ear, "Women use it to develop their...you know, bosom!"

Henry blushed, "Do you use one of these?"

Lily sat up straight and thrust her chest out, "Why, do you think I need to?"

Henry winked and smiled, "You know I like you just the way you are."

"Ah gees, I haven't ever heard of such a thing," Jake grabbed the directions as the Princess Bust Developer made it around the table. He read "a new scientific help to nature. If nature hasn't flattered you with that greatest charm, a full and rounded bosom, use the Princess!" Jake squinted at the directions in his left hand, and held his right hand out in the form of the cup. "I think this works just as well!" He continued to read, "The Princess comes in two sizes, four inch and five inch, the four inch developer is the most popular...and the most desirable!!!"

Everyone enjoyed the laugh and as things settled down Henry put up his hands to regain control. "There is more in this box from the Drug Emporium." Henry reached in the box and held up two syringes and two glass tubes, one filled with morphine, the other with heroine!

Chapter 9

Friday June 8, 1906

The mournful wail of a distant train whistle woke Tony. The left side of his face was buried in the pillow and his right eye squinted at his Alaska Silver pocket watch on the night stand, it read six AM. He slowly rolled over and stared at the ceiling fan. "A Friday to remember, maybe even tell his kids about someday. Thoughts of Vera Dobbs departed as he slowly rose out of bed. The only plan for the morning was a breakfast meeting with Jake and Tommy. Tony performed his morning routine and headed downstairs for breakfast. When he arrived at the trio's favorite table, he stopped and scratched his head. "There is something seriously wrong here! Waiter!"

The waiter came running to the table. "What is the matter Mr. Taylor?"

"Who are these men at my table?"

"Why, it is Mr. Shaw and Mr. Balas. Are you feeling alright Mr. Taylor?"

"Yes I am, these two look familiar, but they are dressed like city folks. They actually look good!"

"Yea, thanks to Cletus. After you said we needed a little fixing up in the wardrobe department, we stopped to see our old friend over at The Plains Toggery." Jake held out his arm. "Silk stuff like you wear Tony, but more like western you know? We can actually get these pant legs down over our boots." Jake seemed quite proud of himself.

"Did you remember to get a jacket to wear?" Tony asked.

Both men nodded respectfully.

"Well then, let's get down to business. I only have a couple things on my mind about this meeting. Who is going to be in charge? Oliver... Tommy? What do you two think?

Jake spoke up first, "I think Oliver should introduce us Tony, but after that you should lead. I mean if we ever get an arrest out of all this, you will be the one in charge."

Tony liked the idea. "How are we doing for money? We have to retain a lawyer yet, and we should have money available to entice these doctors to cooperate. I doubt if they will work for free!"

Shaw was on top of it. "Don't worry about it Tony. We'll be meeting Oliver at the bank before we leave for the country club and he said whatever money we need, he will take care of for now. Besides, I have an account with him so if anything unusual comes up, I can get cash."

Jacob was just thinking out loud, "Not that it makes any difference now, but how much money we got in this already?"

Tommy knew. "My receipts total about a hundred bucks right now. That includes the advance to Ivan. By the time we head back home, I'm thinking around two fifty. You agree Tony?"

"I agree, I don't say it enough, but I hope you two know I appreciate your help. I give my receipts to the County Commissioners and they pay me back, you guys just pay. I hope everything we are doing will be successful and we find the killer. When that happens, Parkston will be proud of you. Now, let's get to the bank, Oliver will be waiting for us."

Oliver Stanton was a shrewd and experienced banker. He had suggested the Parkston trio be at the bank early so he could get to know these men some and then assess their strategy for this important meeting. "Doctors are smart men and make a lot of money. Businessmen are smart men who know how to manipulate people who make a lot of money. I think raising the question of how the girl's body got out of Sioux Falls without an autopsy got Dr. Paulson's attention. Now, where do we go from here?"

Tony was first to speak out, "I think we should push hard for a second autopsy with these two doctors in charge. Leland Cobb said we have no credibility in his town, these doctors can give us that. They can remove the stigma of a small town attempt at a frame-up!"

"Maybe one of us could run over and buy a couple of train tickets so the doctors would feel obligated to go to Parkston."

"That's good Jake." Tommy concurred. "Oliver, could you take some money out of my account and bring it along in an envelope marked expenses? It might help get things going if we need to negotiate a fee." The men all agreed and Jake went for the tickets. They decided it would be best to move quickly so the tickets would be for a departure Saturday morning and a return ticket for Sunday.

Once at the Country Club, Oliver asked for a table at the rear of the restaurant. He didn't want the distraction of people coming and going. When the doctors arrived, Stanton positioned Dr. Paulson between himself and Tommy. Tommy had the envelope with the cash. Seated at Tommy's left was Tony, then Dr. Olson, then Jake, he had the tickets. The meeting began with lunch and small talk. What is Parkston like? How large is it? Does Parkston have a hospital? Tony broke through the chatter. "Have you doctors discussed our question about the Parkston girl's predicament?"

Dr. Paulson, a very deliberate man spoke, "We have, what are the chances of Dr. Olson and me going to Parkston to perform an autopsy of our own on the girl?" A silence descended over the table. Tony looked at Jake and motioned with his eyes and head like, throw out the tickets you dumb shit! Tommy, in anticipation reached his hand into his jacket pocket to get his envelope...Oliver broke the silence. "Pretty damn good I'd say!" Jake tossed the tickets on the table and Tommy pulled the envelope marked "expenses" from his pocket and held it up! All six men enjoyed a good laugh and went about planning how this would all take place. Tony, busy taking notes about what needed to be done, didn't even notice Leland Cobb sit down a couple of tables to there left. Ollie gave Tony a little kick under the table and tilted his head in Cobb's direction. Tony acknowledged with a sly smile.

As the six men concluded their business lunch and were leaving the club, they passed right past Leland Cobb, Tony lagged behind and stopped. Pointing toward the two doctors he rubbed Cobb. "My credibility is walking out the door Leland. By the way, I'm going to see Vera to make that appointment for Monday. I hope late morning works for you!"

Henry Moss on the other hand, was on his own mission this early Friday morning. He was going to relive Agnes's last day so help him God. He arrived at Sorenson's house a little past seven am;"you up there Vilas?"

"I'm up here Mossy." Henry scurried up the stairs to the room facing east toward the Wiseman house. "Good morning Vilas, I brought you a little present if you don't mind."

"I do mind! You don't have to go buying me nothing Henry…what did you get me?"

"I didn't mean to snoop, but I see you collect model train cars. This isn't much, I hope you like them." Henry handed him the box and then irresistibly moved to the window to watch the Wiseman house. It was as if he thought he might see Agnes working outside and this would all have been nothing but a bad dream.

"I'll be damned Mossy, where did you find this?" The box contained six model cars of an US Army supply train. The engine, and each car after including the caboose, had a 7th Cavalry insignia painted on the side.

"I found an Army Surplus store downtown. I got myself a set too; I think I'll start collecting."

"Well thank you son, I didn't get you anything!" Vilas laughed.

"You helping me with this investigation is worth more than any gift I could ever buy for you." Returning to the window Henry asked, "Is this about the time of the morning you came up here last Friday?"

Sorenson put the toy cars on the floor and wheeled over to the window beside Henry. "Yes, same time. Hot like this morning too."

"What did you see first?"

"The first thing I noticed was there was a buggy out back."

"Did you know who the buggy belonged too?"

"Don't know, or I should say I didn't know until later. You see the buggy was there when I got here so it had to have been there before seven thirty…that's when I got here last Friday morning."

"So did you find out who the buggy belonged to?"

"It belonged to a doctor, I seen him there a few times, most always when Walter was away. I don't know his name."

"What happened next?"

"He left; I guess around eight thirty because I usually take a pee around that time. You

know, it takes awhile to take a leak when you're in a chair. I guess I got back here to my post about fifteen minutes later. I wanted to be here because after what I saw the night before, I figured something was going to happen."

"Did it?"

"It did! But not till after eleven. I know it was after eleven because I just got back here from peeing again. Don't laugh; you're not old enough to know what it's like! Anyway, the same doctor in the same buggy pulls up and he goes right into the house. Maybe fifteen minutes or so later, an ambulance pulls up."

"Was it an ambulance or a hearse?"

"Both I guess, NOBLE FUNERAL PARLOR it said on the side of it.

"Who was driving the ambulance, did you know him?"

Vilas looked up with a scowl, "Henry, why would you think I would know him? I didn't know who the doctor was, how would I know who the ambulance driver was. All I know is they went inside with a stretcher and came out with a body about fifteen minutes later. Then, when the doctor was giving the driver instructions he looked kind of upset. He pointed south and the driver sped off south. The doctor paced around some with his hand on his hips, then got in his buggy and followed."

"Where did they go?"

"Mossy, in case you haven't noticed in the past few days, I am in a wheelchair. How the hell would I know? You have the legs, go find out!"

"Ding-dang it, don't get all bucky with me! You know I raise horses for a living, I'm not a detective! I just thought maybe you knew where this funeral parlor is so I could go find the driver."

"I don't need an undertaker yet, but the only hospital in that direction is Southside General. It would make sense this funeral home would be down there, people die in hospitals. Just go south out of here about a mile and then right on Western Avenue. That will take you right to the hospital."

Henry followed his direction to the hospital and sure as heck the Noble Funeral Parlor was right there. Henry went in the front door. "Hello...anyone around?"

"How may I help you sir?"

"Gees, you startled me mister. Sorry, I guess I'm a bit jumpy about places like this."

"You shouldn't be. You appear to be alive."

"Yea, so far I am. My name is Henry Moss, from Parkston. I, ah, I was wondering if I could speak to your ambulance driver. It seems he picked up a friend of mine last week Friday and delivered her to that hospital."

"Are you with the police? I am sorry, forgive my manners...my name is Hubert Schnell, I drive the ambulance"

I am pleased to meet you Hubert Schnell." The two men shook hands as Henry explained the situation. "So that is why I am trying to track down what happened to Agnes last Friday, the local DA and his people apparently do not want anything to do with it."

Schnell grabbed Henry's arm and kind of steered him towards the side door which opened to an alley way where a couple of wagons were parked. "I am sorry, but my boss was coming in the other door and he would surely have wanted to know what was going on. I was there last Friday, at the Wiseman house, I told him that what he was doing was wrong."

"Who did you tell?"

"Dr. Downing."

"What did you tell this Downing?"

"That the girl deserved an autopsy. I am the one who picked her up at the Wiseman house. Delivered her there, Hubert pointed to the hospital. I think it was about noon when I got her there, she was beat up pretty bad...but she was alive! Nurse Ellie took care of her the best she could. Downing didn't seem to care much."

"Downing is the doctor who was at the house."

"Yes, Calvin Downing. He called me to the house Friday morning. The girl...what was her name?"

"Agnes, Agnes Kreutzer, from Parkston."

"I will tell you this Henry Moss. The conditions at that house were horrible. Anyway, we got Agnes on the stretcher and down the stairs to the ambulance. I heard Downing mumble something. I think he said he would prefer this was a hearse. But Agnes was a fighter. You know, I have not spoken to Ellie all this week. You really should talk to her you know?"

"Can you help me Hubert?" Henry sensed he was getting close to something.

Hubert thought a moment about Downing getting him fired. "What the hell, I haven't had my coffee break yet. Let's get over to the hospital."

The two men walked the short distance in silence, each thinking what to do next. Hubert led the way around to the rear entrance where the buggies were parked. "Good, Downing's buggy is not here. Nurse Ellie should be around admissions this time of the morning. Yes, there she is." Hubert caught her eye and waved her over. She waved back but signaled it would be one minute.

"It was just last Friday that all this happened Mr. Moss, how is it you are here investigating in just one week?"

"It was all pretty suspicious so we performed our own autopsy!"

"Damn good one, I knew I was right!"

"Hi Hubie, what are you so excited about?"

"Ellie, this is Henry Moss, from Parkston, he is here asking some questions about a patient of yours last week. I brought her in about noon last Friday."

"It is nice to meet you Mr. Moss and of course I remember her, her name was Esther I believe?"

Henry removed his hat and nodded to Ellie, "Actually her name was Agnes, Agnes Kreutzer."

"Oh, well Dr. Downing must have been confused because he checked her in with the name Esther. The doctor said she had suffered from vertigo and taken several bad falls."

Hubert, "Henry did an autopsy, he thinks she was murdered. He is following leads because the police here won't."

"That's right ma'am. I am trying to piece together that Friday. What was the procedure after you first saw Agnes?"

Ellie was concerned about this talk of a murder, "she was an emergency of course so we took her down to an examining room to clean her wounds and get a decent gown for her. She had been sedated and was definitely alive."

"Was Dr. Downing there for all of this?" Henry asked.

"Yes, we were both with her for the examination. Then he gave her more sedative and left."

"When did Agnes die?"

Ellie looked down at the floor, then back up to Henry. "She died early that same afternoon. That is when I called Hubert. I thought she was going to make it Mr. Moss. I guess her wounds were worse than I thought. But the doctor said her wounds were accidental, if she was beaten…I can't imagine who could have done such a thing."

"That is what we are trying to find out and with your help we are getting closer to the truth."

Henry left the hospital and had one more stray pony to get back in the corral before he could go join his friends at Lily's place. This strays name was Nate Bumpers.

Vilas said Bumpers usually did chores around the Wiseman house later in the day and sure enough there he was. Henry rode in slow as not to spook the lad.

"What do you want now Moss?"

Henry just coaxed his pony in a circle around and around Nate, then dismounted. "I have been waiting for this moment Bumpers and I would appreciate it very much if you just stand there and listen without letting that mouth of yours go off. If you look close at the back of your pocket watch you will see that it has three initials imprinted on it…HWM, Henry Weaver Moss, me! You see I gave that watch to Agnes as a going away present before she came over here. She really liked the watch Bumpers, said she would keep it with her forever. Now she's dead and you have it. If you don't start telling me the truth about what happened here last week, two things are going to happen to you, both bad! First, I am going to kick your young ass till there is blood coming out of every opening in your body. Second, while you lay there on the ground bleeding, I'll drag you over to that tree, tie you up, and go get the sheriff. He can arrest you for the murder of Agnes Kreutzer!" Henry reached up and yanked the rope from his saddle!

"NO…no Moss. Listen to me, I can help you, I may have pushed Agnes around some but it was only because Ruth was beating her. Honest, I only tried to help. I could be your witness, yea, I can help you, here, take your watch back."

"You saw her beat Agnes?"

"Oh yea, ever since the little Wiseman girl died she beat all the girls that came to work here. Why do you think Walter got your girl from way out there in immigrant land to work here? There isn't a local girl will come within a hundred yards of this place. Another thing Moss, that box of drugs you got, I seen you buy it off that delivery boy yesterday. I can tell you all about what they were used for!"

Henry backed off; he had gotten what he came for. "You will testify to what you seen happen around here Bumpers?"

"If it saves me, of course I will."

"Well, we will try to keep the law off you once this all breaks open, now give me that watch back before I kick your ass just to make me thirsty!"

Chapter 10

Saturday June 9, 1906

The southbound three o'clock train from Mitchell chugged into the teeth of a twenty mile per hour wind, a pretty calm day by prairie standards. The train of course weighed more so it was right on schedule as it moaned and gasped for air and water. The massive iron locomotive slowly came to rest at the Parkston station and let out one huge fart of pent up steam. With that blast out of the way, Gubby Rausch hustled over to the first class passenger car with a step stool and passengers departed, holding on to their bonnets and hats as the wind swirled around the platform.

"Baggage carts are coming in at the second door on your right, give us about five minutes and they will all be unloaded." Gubby greeted each passenger and made a few mental notes about each one he didn't know. "Hmm, the Parkston gang has returned home with some guests it appears." Mr. Taylor, Jacob and Tommy are escorting two distinguished looking men toward the bag room. "I'll need to check my roster to see who they are."

Tommy led the men across East Main to the shady side of the street. "Unlike your fine city of Sioux Falls, the towns up and down this rail line all got off to the same start. Well, Parkston was a little unique in that we were originally called Dakota City. The town was built where the early settlers thought the rail line would pass, two miles southeast of here. The line missed them so they just moved the town here. We have a few problems but I like to think these local business folks have done pretty well."

Tony interrupted and pointed to the big elevator dominating the scene, "Tommy's being a little modest. That grain elevator over there, the tallest one of those five, is Tommy Shaws. It overshadows the whole town!"

Jake stepped in front of the men and held the door open for them. "Here we are Doctors, the St. Charles Hotel. Clifford over there at the front desk has your rooms ready I'm sure."

Cliff registered the two doctors from Sioux Fall in rooms on either side of his large suite on the third floor. Tony Taylor would occupy the suite and use it to entertain the men at a reception in their honor this evening. "Thank you very much for help Cliff. I think we should allow these gentlemen to get settled in their quarters. I hope I am not out of line doctors, but I have arranged for a small gathering for cocktails at approximately five thirty. The guests of honor would of course be you two, and we will be joined by Doctor Hughes and Zachary Rothe. They performed the original autopsy. Tommy and Jacob will also join us. Cliff will serve hors d'oeuvres and cocktails will be served by our friend Ben Miller. Please, enjoy your stay with us."

Tony and Cliff backed themselves rather clumsily out of the hallway and into the suite. "All right Cliff, what's been going on around here the past few days?"

"It has been pretty quiet. Most of the talk is about the money the town will lose if that brewery doesn't get built. People want to know if Wiseman is the culprit. Marion comes in for coffee and we talk, but we didn't have much to talk about till you guys got back with these doctors. This is a good break for us not?"

"It is a good break for us. We have a lot to do to get prepared for this autopsy. These men are tops in their field. Paulsen graduated from Johns Hopkins University, can you believe it?" Tony was going at top speed and Cliff just rolled his eyes and thought, "what the hell is a Johns Hopkins University?"

"The doctors gave us a list of things they will need from us to get this done right. Doc and I can go over it together. They say they brought all the medical instruments they need with them. All we need to provide is a quiet, well ventilated room with light. We need to keep the group small, three or four should do it. I think Marion needs to be in on this. We will certainly need his help through it all. Do you know if Henry Moss is back? He helped get the body there the first time."

"I thought Ben said he was coming back on the train. He's supposed to be bringing the Kreutzers to the reception tonight. Gee, look at what time it is, I got to get to work on the food for the party. By the way Tony, where is this autopsy thing going to take place?"

"Don't know, we will have to find a place soon though."

The Saturday night crowd was filling Main Street outside but it was quiet conversation in the third floor suite at the St. Charles Hotel. Food and drink was plentiful and the atmosphere was calm as Henry Moss escorted Lily, John and Christine into the room.

"Henry, bring the folks over here, I want to introduce them to the Doctors." It was Tony calling and Henry obeyed. Tony introduced everyone and discreetly let the Doctors assure John and Christine that everything would be fine. It was critical to find out what happened to Agnes, and a second autopsy done by them would help do that.

Lily and Henry mingled some and returned a few minutes later to meet Paulsen and Olson. Although the two doctors were not familiar with the FOUR LEAF CLOVER SALOON, they were very cordial and seemed genuinely interested in getting to know everyone. "So Mr. Moss, you raise horses on your farm. I suppose you have heard the automobile is coming very soon, what will you do then?"

Henry was patient as Lily smiled at him and went to sit with Jake and his wife Angela. "Actually I buy and sell ponies mostly. But I do keep a few horses in stock for the local farmers. You see horses are for working while ponies are for riding. I guess I'll probably keep more horses around though. We will need them to pull all those automobiles out of the mud!" Both doctors gave a cordial little chuckle.

"I do have a question for both of you if you don't mind." Henry pulled the small box of drugs he had bought at the Wiseman house out of his jacket pocket. "What do you make of this?"

Olsen and Paulsen studied the contents of the box, syringes, morphine and heroine. "Where did you get this Mr. Moss?"

"I bought it from a courier in Sioux Falls"

"So they are selling it on the streets. I guess there is nothing illegal about that is there Olson?"

"No, there isn't. You probably haven't seen much of this around Parkston Henry, but unfortunately it is becoming a popular drug of choice in Sioux Falls and other cities. This heroine, it actually started out being touted as God's own gift to medicine, morphine! People were, and still are, being duped into believing it is a cure all. If you have pain, morphine can stop it, because it will numb that pain to the satisfaction of the user. Problem is it is extremely addictive. That is even worse," Olsen held up the box as others had gathered around to listen. "This is heroine. About eight years ago drug companies started to advertise this as a cough medicine. Many diseases will make you cough, sometimes violently. Heroine will stop that cough so in the user's mind stop the disease! Problem is, it to is addictive. A medical journal article I read recently says there may be as many as a million heroine addicts in America today. Oh, one other problem with these boxes, they have no instructions! Do you shoot yourself full with one syringe or both?" I don't know how to answer your question Henry, but I think it would be safe to say whoever was buying this could very well be addicted to it!"

"I hate to interrupt the good doctors; this is all so very interesting. The world around us is changing so fast. But we have reached a decision as to when and where the autopsy will be. If you will gather around we can tell you..........."

The autopsy would be done in the old meat locker only a half a block from the hotel. There was no disrespect meant in choosing the site, but the morgue was out because there would be services at the Catholic Church across the street and access to it would be limited. The locker was large, clean, and well lit, and it would be easy to get a gurney in and out. The autopsy could begin early before most citizens would be going to church, and should be completed before services at all the churches ended around noon. There was a town meeting scheduled for early afternoon. If things went according to plan, the concerned people of Parkston would find out if all of the work in Sioux Falls this past week had paid off, and if it had, who was going to pay for it.

Chapter 11

Sunday June 10, 1906

It was seven AM and Henry had his wagon backed up to the alley entrance of the locker plant. Doc Hughes was there to help and the casket was wheeled in for what would hopefully be the girl's last disturbance. Her body was carefully removed and placed on a large wood block-like table in the middle of the room. Paulsen and Olsen called on Denton Noble to identify the body as the same one he sent to Parkston over a week ago. Denton said it was the same girl and the doctors continued. Others present were Marion Campbell, Zach Rothe, Jacob, Tony and Tommy. Zachary would be the note taker and Hughes would be right up front to assist.

"I just want you two to know I really appreciate you letting me be here. Zachary and I did the best we could under the circumstances and I am ready for any criticism you have for me. I only want to learn from the best. Oh, also be careful when you get around the table, there is a small gutter in the concrete floor that carries the blood of the animals away while the butcher works. I just didn't want either of you to trip in it."

"Dr. Olsen and I are pleased to be here. We hope we can be of help in determining what caused the death of this young woman. It is unfortunate that we could not have visited this issue at the time of her death in Sioux Falls. There was apparently some sort of mix up. If we could have performed the autopsy then, we would have had body fluids and probably access to where this unfortunate girl spent the last few hours of her young life. We will begin our work with a simple observation of the general condition of the body."

The observers in the room were mesmerized as the two doctors went to work. One on each side, they circled the cadaver in a clockwise direction, neither one speaking. It was almost as if each man knew what the other was thinking. If one moved to adjust the body for a closer look, the other responded on cue. Round and round they went. Then they stepped back across the gutter, crossed their arms across their chest, and paused for what seemed an eternity to Hughes. He waited for some comment on his work. He got none.

Paulson spoke first..."The blow to the right side of her head was definitely not from a fall. If it was from a fall, the cut would be upward. This cut is a downward slice."

Olson. "I agree. I think the attacker was perhaps left-handed and about the same height as the victim. All of these wounds probably contributed to her death... You are writing this down aren't you?"

"Yes, keep going."

Paulsen, "These broken fingers on the right hand and the damage to her right shoulder may indicate she was fighting back."

Olsen, "What do you make of the wounds on her back?"

Paulsen, "Puncture wounds of some kind, not a knife, a pointed instrument. Do you think we're ready to open?"

Olsen, "Yes, but we had discussed asking them about, you know. Maybe we should do it now."

Paulsen, "You're right. Could Doctor Hughes and Mr. Rothe meet us to the side please?"

The entire audience was surprised and Zachary and Doc nearly fainted. "What could we have done wrong?"

They met off in the shadows to right, out of sight to the audience. "We didn't mean to startle you. Everything is fine. Your work is most commendable. Your incisions seem to be very accurate and should allow us to move along at a quick pace. We have but one question for you Doctor Hughes. We apologize for not asking it before we got to this far." The doctors needed to know if the pubic region of the girl had been inspected for signs of rape. They did not want to perform this part of the autopsy in front of an audience if it had already been completed. They were confident in Hughes's ability and would trust his opinion.

Hughes was relieved and whispered, "We did that inspection. We found no signs of rape or bruising on the girl."

The autopsy was completed in a couple of hours and the doctors returned to the hotel to clean up and change clothes. Their train did not leave for Sioux Falls till later in the afternoon so they would be guests at the street rally. The young girl's body was replaced in her casket and returned to the cemetery for her third interment. This time she was buried without her heart or brain. They were placed in jars of formaldehyde and could be used as evidence in any impending trial.

At the same time the Sunday events in Parkston were unfolding, Walter Wiseman, Judge Acres and Dr. Downing were meeting at Walter's house in Sioux Falls to sort things out. Walter and Ruth had returned home from Sioux City just the night before. "Leland Cobb says some men from Parkston have been poking around asking questions. It seems they did their own autopsy and think there is something to investigate."

Walter just sat there motionless except for the rolling of his coffee cup between his two hands. He slowly sat the cup aside. "What's your take on this Judge?"

Acres scratched his head, "Leland told them their accusations were useless here. They have no credibility in this city. I suspect they will go about getting some kind of credibility here. I hear they retained Kirby Johnson to help out."

Walter responded with a smile. "That pettifogger, if the DA from Hutchinson County isn't any smarter than that, things may just go away. You know you can put the coffee pot down Calvin. I think we are done with it."

"Sorry Walter. I think there is something you should know about. Leland told us that he saw the Parkston gang having lunch with Doctors Paulson and Olson at the club on Friday. Leland doesn't know what they were talking about, but he thought they might be arranging another autopsy. Do you think they would ship the body back here?"

Walter rose from his chair and slowly walked to the window. He thought about the past few days in Sioux City. Ruth had never mentioned anything that would make him doubt the fact that Agnes died from horrible disease. What about the vertigo the girl suffered from? What about the falling down the stairs or her anemia? Why would these people from Parkston question this death? "Calvin, I think Ruth may need some water, would you be kind enough to take a pitcher up to her?"

"Certainly Walter, I should be checking on her anyway." Downing poured some water in a pitcher, placed it on a tray with a couple of glasses and made his way to the hallway. Once outside the kitchen he paused to hear what Frank and Walter would talk about.

Walter put his index finger to his mouth, signaling to Frank to keep quiet. Moments passed before the men heard the creak of the steps as Calvin finally made his way up the stairs.

"Frank, I'm confused about all of this and I'm never confused about anything. Why are the people in Parkston, many of them friends of mine, questioning what happened to Agnes?"

"I don't know."

"It's always been about me Frank, the money, the work always came first. I've done well that's for sure, but at what cost? When Emmalena died I grieved for a couple days and went back to work. It was all I knew how to do. I would be on the road for weeks at a time. Ruth loathed me for that. She told me that when we were in Sioux City. She said I could run around the country selling my beer and all she could was sit at home with the thoughts of her dead child and drink that beer! That's what she said Frank. When Ruth and I were in Sioux City, we went to a sanitarium. You know she drinks like crazy when I'm not around and I've even heard from some neighbors that she may even do worse things. So I checked her in. She was not pleased about it, but she went, she hasn't spoken but a couple of times since she got out. When she does, she asks about Agnes. Ruth says she was alive the last time she saw her."

"Walter, do you think she will get stronger? We don't know what is going on out there. It is possible there could be an investigation."

Walter thought long and hard before he spoke, "This is all so foreign to me Frank. For the first time since I can remember, I am not in control. You and I need to keep in very close touch the next couple of days and I don't think we should involve Calvin in our plans."

Church goers in Parkston would have normally been home by one o'clock on a Sunday afternoon, but today, rural and town folk alike gathered at the intersection of Main Street and First Avenue for a town meeting to get information about this alleged murder. People wanted to know what was true and not true. Rumors were all around, some saying this investigation and possible trial could cost the city thousands of dollars. Who would pay for it? Some say, including the mayor, that it could bankrupt the city! The mayor was also concerned about the rumors saying Ruth Wiseman killed the girl. If those rumors persist, Wiseman may renege on his warehouse plans. He already has four full time carpenters working on it and there could even be a brewery here someday. That would mean a lot of jobs for a small town! Finally, the crowd quieted and the mayor got to speak. Well, try to anyway.

"Welcome to Parkston, all of you, here today. We have a lot to talk about and we need to inform you about some issues that have arisen after the death of a young girl, Agnes…Mayor Kepler turned to his village council chief Dormier. "What the hell was her name?"

"Kreutzer, Agnes Kreutzer, her parents are sitting right over there!

"Okay then, we are gathered here to try and figure out what we can do as a town to help, or as many of us feel, if we should do anything at all." Kepler was not a good speaker. Crowds made him nervous, and this crowd, numbering close to a hundred people, was more than he had anticipated. The common thought around town was that if it was a Catholic girl who died, let the Catholics pay, or the county. The mayor didn't understand the opportunity that was at hand. This town had grown despite itself. The many churches were always at odds about things, mostly who would pay for city improvements. There was one man on the platform who knew exactly what to say, Marion Campbell. The local editor, the man who had his finger on the pulse of this town, had been watching it slowly tear itself apart for to many years and understood precisely why. To Marion, the ambiguity was clear. To the hundred or so Methodists, Baptists, Lutherans, Presbyterians, German Lutherans, Catholics and Mayor Kepler, it all seemed so ambiguous.

The last straw for Marion, the reason he felt compelled to speak, was that he understood the fact that most of these people didn't give a damn that this girl was murdered. It so happened that he and Frankie had put a "feeler" out to each of the area churches asking their church leaders to let their parish know that the Kreutzer family would need help financially to find out what happened to their daughter. He had asked, that because of the urgency of the matter, they would do it at their respective church services this very morning, and then either he or Frankie would contact them to see how much support each church would give. Father Mullaney from the church Agnes attended, the Catholic Church, was the only yea! They would support the girl's family in any way possible!

Marion asked the mayor if he could have a word with the people. The mayor gladly obliged.

"I think most of you know me, I'm Marion Campbell. I own and am the editor of the PARKSTON PROGRESS. Did you know that there are approximately nine hundred people living in Parkston?" Marion paused as the crowd rustled around a bit feeling good about them selves. "Did you ever stop to count the number of churches in this town? There are nine. Nine churches for nine hundred people. If you draw a circle around Parkston, say six miles in each direction, there are another two hundred people; we are growing are we not?" The crowd cheered, yes! Yes! "You can add another seven country churches to the list! That makes eleven-hundred people and sixteen churches!" the crowd was quiet, not knowing how to respond.

Campbell continued, "The honorable mayor simply overlooked some people on the platform here I would like to recognize. John and Christine Kreutzer and little Gracie are seated up here. It is Agnes, there sixteen year old daughter who is the focal point of this meeting." Somewhat embarrassed, they give a little wave.

"The two distinguished gentlemen on my left are Doctors Paulson and Olsen; I will explain why they are here in a minute. And seeing as I know what most of you think of this situation we are facing as a town, I would like to draw your attention to Elmer and David Schmidt, two of our Hutchinson County Commissioners, I think they are the only two here today. Is that right Elmer? Yes? Anyway, just so you know, the commissioners have voted to fund the investigation of the death of Agnes Kreutzer!"

It was like a huge worry was lifted from the crowd and they cheered wildly. Men standing around the commissioners patted their backs and shook their hand, "Hooray, hooray for Hutchinson County!" The crowd was actually saying, "We are so glad you did it because we weren't going to."

Marion surveyed the crowd as most of them cheered, not all of them, and that got his hopes up. He knew, and agreed with the minority that it was time this town stood up for one of their own. Crowds are funny, the Catholics crowded together to Campbell's right. The Lutherans took up most of the middle, and Baptists and other Protestants filled in his left.

As the crowd settled down, Marion took his shot. "We took a little straw poll this morning at various local church services. Some of you may have talked to me, or Frankie, some of you not. We asked if you would be willing to help the Kreutzer family financially as we all try to find out how their daughter died. Well, the results are in, and in light of the news from our commissioners, Frankie and I thought you might be interested in knowing those results; would you?"

The mayor had now turned into somewhat of a cheer leader. "Yes, of course we would!"

"Alright, I'm glad you said that Mayor. Apparently, being in a church no sooner makes you a Christian than being in a pig barn makes you a pig!" The crowd gasped. "This TOWN, and I emphasize TOWN, of Parkston has voted. The number of churches who stepped up front to help is, an overwhelming ONE!" Marion paused for a few seconds to let the crowd shuffle around a little and mumble to the person standing next to him. Some people were embarrassed or mad and started to leave, Marion showed no mercy. "Don't leave people, I'm just getting started! Drs. Olsen and Paulson here, while most of you were in church this morning pretending, performed a second autopsy on Agnes. Their findings confirm our Dr. Hughes's opinion that Agnes was brutally murdered. Can you walk away from that? God bless Hutchinson County, but should we let them pay our way? I was going to write all of this in an editorial for Thursday's paper, and I still will so my words are not blown away by the prairie wind. But by then I'm afraid it would be too late. So, I am going to tell you what I think right now."

Clarence Van shouted. "In Europe the government took our money and put us in the army. I pay my taxes, but I want my money to go to the Baptist Church. We don't need the government!" Clarence got applause from those folks around him.

Marion let the crowd settle down and walked to the edge of the platform and addressed the man, "Then I guess that would make you a Baptist and an Anarchist Clarence!"

"I am a newspaper man. I know what goes on here and around the world. I know about POGRAMS. I know that Christians and Jews in Europe have slaughtered each other for hundreds of years. A little over two years ago Easter and the Passover fell on the same day. In one Russian city alone over a hundred Jews were murdered in the street because they got in the way of Easter. Christ's resurrection from death to eternal life. Unless God has a miracle in store for us on this vast prairie, Agnes Kreutzer will simply be remembered as the girl from Parkston who was murdered, then dug up from her grave not once, but twice, to prove that she was murdered, and then forgotten because no one gave a damn about the fact that she was one of our own."

"You people disgust me. You live in the past. You live your lives here the same way your parents lived their lives in Europe, hating everything foreign to your way; Protestant or Catholic. Think about it. This community, no, strike that out. We are not a community, we are just a town. Webster says a community is a group living in an area sharing......sharing common ideas and interests. He defines a town as a concentration of houses, somewhat larger than a village. We are eleven hundred people and sixteen churches in a six mile circle. That is all Parkston is."

Casper Bork, owner of a lumber yard in town shouted up to Marion, "word on the street is that Walter Wiseman's wife is your main suspect. If you go after her, Walter would renege on his warehouse. He could be the future of this town!" Casper got some applause.

"So what your saying Casper, is that if Ruth Wiseman did murder our Agnes, we should not go after her because Walter Wiseman can put money in our pockets? This town needs an identity but I don't think that's it!" Marion was winning some of the crowd over.

"Twenty years ago, The Great Iron Horse Train came roaring up the tracks from Yankton, birthing little towns along the way. Tyndall, Scotland, Kaylor, Tripp, Beardsley, Parkston, Dimock, Ethan...like babies, we all started with the same things. Instead of fingers and toes, we had coal bins and water towers. Instead of a brain to function with, we had a depot to tell us where to get on or off. Like children, we grew up different. Some got bigger, stronger, some died. Why do some siblings do better than others? Because they take advantage of opportunities along the way. They make right decisions; they learn do the right thing! Now, we are at a crossroads. Every Sunday you go to your church and visit with people who think like you and act like you, and you talk about all the bad things your neighbors do because they are this or that. You have your blinders fit perfectly on your head and you go live out your week feeling all good about yourself. We are at a crossroads. History tells us that in order to be a great country you must survive a civil war. Slavery propelled America into our civil war and America survived. We expanded and grew and now we flex our muscles around the world, a unified people. Let the murder of Agnes Kreutzer propel Parkston into its own Civil War. Let us tear at her and fight the fact that she was a catholic over and over in our minds…and then, if we can get over it, we will have survived our civil war. We can be united in the fact that she is simply one of us and can go on to great heights as a community that did the right thing."

Marion looked out at all those blank faces and realized that they were doing exactly what he asked. They were fighting all those age old demons in their minds, fighting their own individual civil war. He could see the blinders coming off. He rejoiced inside as a Lutheran took a Catholic hand and shook it. He rejoiced as a Catholic took a Baptist hand and shook it.

Marion struck again. "Join me people. Join me up here. Pick up the Parkston Banner and hold it high in the air! Pick up the shield with the Kreutzer family crest on it, and let it protect us on our crusade for justice against the Queen City Sioux Falls!"

It was a Sunday to remember in Parkston, and in Hutchinson County. The people celebrated their metamorphosis from a town to a community with a party that lasted well into the evening. The mayor lifted the no alcohol on Sunday ban and local bar keepers rolled out free kegs of beer and root beer. The band played patriotic songs and people dug deep into their wallets and purses to help the cause. Churches donated their offering plates to the cause. Children were hoisted up on daddy's shoulders and dropped coins into boxes set out on the platform as they paraded by. Word spread and people that hadn't even heard Campbell's speech jumped in line to help. People who just arrived in town on the afternoon train, people just passing through, got in the line and dropped nickels in the box. The depot master would later say he heard these passengers say as their train departed, "what a great little city, we must come back here again!"

It would be a great send off for the people representing the town and the county in Sioux Falls. People like Tony Taylor and Jake Balas were put on the platform and waved to the crowd. Tommy Shaw even coaxed Henry Moss up there much to the delight of Lily and her girls. But the highlight of the afternoon was when John and Christine Kreutzer were wheeled out in a wagon quickly, and rather poorly, transformed into a float of sorts. The people didn't care, they cheered. They felt more pride when John thanked them all and Grace and Christine shyly waved and smiled. Then, Henry and Lily climbed on with the two girls and they followed the band in a parade to the train station for the start of the crusade. People marched behind the wagon singing:

Parkston will shine tonight, Parkston will shine
When the sun goes down and the moon comes up
Parkston will shine!

"Well chief, you certainly turned this town around, congratulations!" Frankie was all excited about the day. "Aren't you going to the train station?"

Marion looked a bit exhausted from the day. "No, you go ahead and keep an eye on things. You know Frankie; in real life, most of those crusaders got slaughtered when they reached the battle field!"

Chapter 12

Monday June 11, 1906

Gubby Rausch should be depot master of the month for The Chicago and St. Paul Western Railroad. The early train leaving Parkston for Sioux Falls was full of local crusaders. Within an hour after their arrival in Sioux Falls, they had posted several people at five of the busiest intersections in the downtown district.

"Good morning, I am from Parkston, South Dakota. It is a small community out in what city folks call immigrant land. I am here hoping you could spare a nickel to help find who killed our Agnes. She was murdered in your city and the police here won't help us." It was a simple plan with two goals, one to raise money for the cause, and two, to peak the Sioux Falls resident's awareness of a heinous crime possibly committed by one of their own citizens. A day earlier, these people from Parkston didn't know, or even care about Agnes Kreutzer. But here they are determined to help! It went very slowly at first, but as word traveled up and down these streets at the height of a busy Monday lunch hour, the clink, clink, clink of thirty or so nickels landing in thirty or so tin cups became quite noticeable.

Aside from the street corner solicitors, Parkston men stood in front of each of the three local newspapers volunteering any information to anyone who might want to write about the case. They also had a few in front of the building that Leland Cobb's office was in. They would talk to pedestrians that passed and say things like, "We are from Hutchinson County, and our district attorney is working hard on finding a killer while yours sits in his office doing nothing!" Then they would peer into the windows and point. It was funny because Cobb's office was several floors above them, but it was entertaining and they did draw the crowd they wanted.

Earlier that Monday morning, well before the train load of Parkston soldiers arrived in his city, Walter Wiseman had decided he needed to go to work. It had always been his refuge from reality and as he drove his buggy through the early morning Sioux Falls streets, he saw none of the diversions he would see on his way home. Quietly he named the buildings and businesses as he past by them..."Elmendorf Meat Packers, Burns Bakery, I helped fund all of them. This has been my town for nearly twenty years! I just don't understand why there is so much interest in this immigrant child?" Soon, he would find out.

Henry Moss was feeling good about himself. His relationship with Lily had rebounded nicely and that helped him concentrate on his assignment for today. Tony was a little nervous about how the next couple of days would unfold so he sent Henry out to talk to his witnesses and just remind them that it was not over yet, they all need to be vigilant. That first class car train ride back to Sioux Falls was nice, but the feel of his favorite pony under him was pure excitement. A flat out, fast as Coffee could go ten block sprint through several somewhat crowded intersections was just what Moss needed to get some focus. It was a couple minutes past nine when Henry arrived in a cloud of dust at Denton Noble's Funeral Parlor. Henry tied his pony to a buggy out back. "Hope you enjoyed that ride as much as I did girl," Henry gave Coffee a big pinch of sugar and went in search of Hubert.

"Over here Henry, I have a wagon full of caskets to unload."

Never one to shirk, Henry pitched in to help.

"Thanks for the help Henry. How did things go back in Parkston?"

"You see your boss yet?"

"No, he is supposed to be helping me with this shipment but I guess he is inside working on something. That's why I'm asking you what happened in Parkston."

"We think things went pretty well. The doctors seemed to agree with our thoughts on what happened and Denton gave a positive identification that Agnes was the girl you sent to Parkston."

"So what is next Henry?"

"Things will be moving at a pretty fast pace the next day or two. Tony Taylor, our district attorney, will be meeting with your Minnehaha guy sometime today. I'm not sure what they all do but they told me to talk to my witnesses and make sure everything is okay. Are you ready for all of this my friend?"

"I am ready! If you are going over to the hospital next, I'd like to go along if you don't mind. I always like to take the opportunity to see Ellie."

"I don't blame you... Yea, let's finish up here and I can tell both of you what my instructions are."

Henry and Hubert were just about ready to leave when Denton hollered at Hubert to come inside. "Looks like the boss needs me to do something, I'll just meet you over there Henry." Henry approached the hospital same as before making sure Downing's buggy was not there, it was not. The instructions he had for his witnesses were simple. Leland Cobb would listen to the evidence and the list of witnesses Tony Taylor had compiled. If he thought the case was strong enough, they would determine what charge to file, get a warrant and then wait for the arrest. The judge will then schedule the preliminary hearing and we will let you know when and where to be as two of our prime witnesses.

"Ellie, you okay with what you saw that day? You said you were with Agnes all the time right?"

"I was with her all the time. Agnes died holding my hand!"

"Alright, we are good to go then. Oh, Tony asked me to tell you not to talk to anyone about any of this, especially newspaper people! Hey, here comes Hubert. Where did you have to go in such a hurry? You had the gravel flying all around with your buggy."

"Denton had a package he needed delivered over to Dr. Paulsen at the Methodist Hospital lab, doing some blood work for an autopsy I guess."

"Anything we need to know about Hubert?"

"I don't think so, Denton didn't seem to be concerned about it, and I was just in a hurry because I wanted to get back here." Ellie, Hubert and Henry sat and talked about the case for awhile concentrating on several different angles. Ellie's main concern was how disappointed she had been because she thought at one point early in the afternoon, Agnes was actually improving. But, it didn't last and soon she was in a coma again.

Downtown, two of the Parkston folks were entertaining a small crowd of Sioux Falls residents with their skit about an inept Leland Cobb when Tony and his assistant Kirby approached the office building. The Parkston men recognized Tony and let out a yell, "Hoorah for Tony Taylor! Give them hell Tony!!" They held the door open for the two lawyers and gave them enthusiastic pats on the back as they passed by. Leland Cobb, less than enthused when Tony tossed the envelope of evidence on his desk, never the less knew what his duty was.

"It's all in there Leland. Two of your cities most prominent doctors say the girl was murdered. We have listed all of the other witnesses we have gathered and their testimony. Here is what we say happened, I hope you agree!"

'You're the boss Tony, open it up and let's get to work!"

John and Christine Kreutzer had arrived in Sioux Falls on a later train. They were frightened by the mood of the crowd as word traveled through the streets about a Jew murderer loose in their city. Henry had given John directions to Lily's place but Christine was frightened by the crowds of people and stayed in their hotel room. It was a few minutes past six o'clock when John joined Henry at Lily's place.

"I have seen crowds like this before Henry, angry crowds in the old country. It is not justice they want, it is bloodshed. It is like Marion said, if there are no Jews around, Catholics and Protestants will fight each other. Now you have a Jew, and if this mob gets a chance, there will be trouble. I thought America would be different, I guess I was wrong."

"It's not the country; it is the people in it. And you don't need Christians and Jews to have one of your pogroms. When I was in the army, I helped clean after one right here in South Dakota. We buried over a hundred native men; women and children who were slaughtered because they wanted to celebrate the Ghost Dance like their ancestors had celebrated. The white army said no, you cannot be like your fathers, they were wrong; you must obey us or die. They continued to celebrate their dance."

"What happened next?"

"The white soldiers placed Gatling guns in a circle around them and opened fire. Within a matter of seconds, most of the natives were dead or dying. Then, a couple of soldiers, muttering something about revenge for Custer, walked among the bodies of the Ghost Dancers and put a bullet in the head of anyone still moving! So you see John, we have our own ways of cleansing. That was Wounded Knee about the same time you were having pogroms in your country. It was winter so we dug a hole as big as we could and tossed all the bodies in, much the same way you tossed the bodies of Jews away I suspect!"

Lily came in and sat down beside Henry. Visibly shaken, she gave Henry a hug.

"What was that for Lily?" Henry was a bit surprised.

"I just came to see you; I am frightened by all of this. I went to see the girls and give them hugs too."

"What is the matter Lily?" John was concerned also.

Lily reached in her bag and tossed a small child's bloody dress on the table. "I took this from a woman on the street today!" Pointing out the front window she continued. "She was right over there. This woman said she was from Parkston and she had a chest full of clothes like this. She held the bloody garments high in the air and waved them about saying they were Agnes Kreutzers clothes. Then she would shout that the poor have no protection from the rich and that poor immigrants suffer all the time and the police do nothing. Someone must help us get the murderer of Agnes Kreutzer. It was horrible."

"Were their people listening to her?"

Distraught, Lily snapped at Henry. "Of course there were! Probably a hundred or so, I don't know. Anyway, I got to the front of the mob somehow and snatched this dress out of the chest." Holding the dress soaked in animal blood out at arms length she continued. "This dress is too small to fit Agnes. What was this woman trying to do?"

Calming Lily down Henry held her hand and explained this woman was only trying to help smoke out the murderer just like they were and that she probably was not even from Parkston. He tried not to let on to John or Lily, but he felt that the bad mood in the street would boil over soon.

Chapter 13

Tuesday, June 12, 1906

Henry Moss poured a cup of coffee and returned the pot to the hot flat stone by the fire pit. On hot summer mornings the men took their coffee outside under the cottonwoods. It was cooler out there and it helped keep the kitchen from heating up the whole house. "I really appreciate you letting me stay here Alex."

"Shucks, it's nothing Henry, you know that. Here it is sun just coming up and I have a cup of coffee all made for me. What time you get in this morning?"

"Just a little while ago, I was…" Henry muttered into his coffee cup. "I was at church most of the night."

"Church! You don't go to church."

"I can't explain it Alex. I left the bar a little after midnight, had plenty to drink, that's for sure. As I passed the Catholic Church that Lily and the girls go to, I remembered something Father Mullaney told me once. I checked the front door and sure enough, it was open. Some lamps were lit and moon light was pouring through the stained glass windows. It all had a very calming effect on me and it felt good being there. So, I went to one of the front pews, knelt down and prayed. It took me a little while to get the hang of it because I hadn't done it for so long. But it came back to me. I asked God to give Agnes peace and to welcome her to Heaven. I asked God for justice here on earth, not for revenge. I prayed that He would simply deliver the killer to the law. I also prayed for myself Alex. All of these years I have thought I was above all this religious rigmarole, I have worked hard to be a good man and to put down roots. Trouble is; those roots don't grow. I asked God to forgive me and bless my life with the Lily and her girls."

"I am proud of you Henry. What happened next?"

"I can't explain it Alex, but a peace of mind came over me. It was so overwhelming that I just curled up in that church pew and slept like a baby. I only slept for a few hours but I feel so good. It is as if God answered my prayer."

"So you think God told the Sheriff to make an arrest today?"

Henry has always had an instinct for impending trouble and thought it over carefully. "If the sheriff makes an arrest today, and I think he will, there will be trouble. This town is all stirred up and a confrontation of some kind will be hard to avoid. Whatever develops Alex will probably be around the court house, that's where the mob will be." Henry paused and scoured the southwest horizon, "Looks like a chance of rain my friend, better wear your rain slicker when the call comes in."

McKenzie caught the wink Henry gave him and knew exactly what he meant. "About what time is this rain coming?"

"Don't know that yet, someone will be by before long to tell us though I expect." Henry was right, not more than an hour had passed when a lone rider approached.

"You hear the news Alex? They arrested Walter Wiseman's wife early this morning. They got her over in the jail now. I got to get over there, going to be a big crowd for the hearing. Yes sir, biggest damn thing around here...maybe ever!"

"What time is the hearing Jack?"

"Eleven o'clock!"

"You got your answer Alex, two and a half hours from now we go to court. Listen, I got a couple things to do around here before I go so meet me in front of Lily's at ten thirty...and bring your gear!"

Henry and Lily stood out front of the saloon and watched the confluence of people in front of the Minnehaha County Courthouse. "Will we be able to get a seat Henry?

"Yea, we can go in with John and Christine. Lily, Alex should be here soon. He's going to help me in case there's trouble getting Wiseman from the jail to the courthouse. I want you to stay here. I'll come back and get you after we know everything is alright...that big crowd over there makes me nervous." Henry disappeared inside for a couple of minutes and then reappeared dressed in a long pale yellow slicker. Alex showed up right on time dressed the same.

The county jail was about a hundred paces across the street from the new courthouse. Why they didn't put them side by side Henry didn't know, would have made to much sense he guessed. If everything went right on schedule and the sheriff had plenty of men to help, everything should be fine. Henry just hoped the sheriff was smart enough to use a wagon. Walking Wiseman across this no man's land, in this case, no woman's land, would be asking for trouble. Two men wearing slickers on a ninety degree morning should draw some attention but it did not, the people outside the courthouse were concentrating too hard on trying to pack four hundred of them into a court room designed to hold only two hundred. This actually worked to Henry and Alex's advantage because they were more interested in the jail.

Henry poked Alex, "Those two men in front of the bakery, big guy and the guy in the straw cowboy hat, you see them?"

"Yea, I see them, who are they?"

"Friends of mine from Parkston, if we need them, they are going to help. Have you seen the sheriff or any deputies yet?"

"No, I haven't...wait Henry, someone is coming out of the jail."

The yellow slickered men stayed twenty or so paces from the front of the jail. "Good, the sheriff was using his head for a change, they did bring a wagon. Now, after they get her up there Alex, we can just shadow them as they make their way towards the big crowd. Alright, here comes a deputy, another deputy and the sheriff with Mrs. Wiseman. Shit, that's it! He only has two on the wagon and three on the ground!"

Henry waved to Jake across the street and signaled five. Jake signaled back that they were ready. The sheriff and his men let Walter ride up top of the wagon with his wife and they started towards the big crowd milling in front of the courthouse. The big Belgian draft horse drawing the wagon could cut his own path through the crowd and things were looking pretty good. The wagon was about half way across the street when McKenzie saw them. A clan of about twenty hooligans all liquored up on Irish whiskey and Wiseman beer appeared from an alley on the left flank of the wagon. Brandishing baseball bats, they attacked. The big Belgian spooked and reared up knocking two of the deputies to the ground.

"This must be some sort of a diversion Henry thought, the main mob was still a hundred and fifty feet away!" Henry was wrong; some of the attackers were holding ropes with nooses at the end. They were intent on capturing the Jewess and have a hanging instead of a trial. Henry held Alex back to see if the sheriff and his men could get across, they couldn't. The sheriff was overwhelmed. One hooligan even got his hands on Ruth's arm and tore the sleeve off her dress as he tried to pull her to the ground. Walter knocked the man down with a big right hand and grabbed the reins. All hell broke loose as the large crowd by the courthouse saw the attack and rushed towards the jail like a herd of thirsty cows smelling water. Feeding off of the violence they were shouting obscenities. "Hang the Jew, get her down from that wagon and string her up!"

Moss and McKenzie sprang into action. Their only chance was to fight off this bunch and get Wiseman back to the jail. They met Tommy and Jake in the middle of the street and fought as a buffer between the big mob and the small one. Alex and Henry ripped open their slickers and tossed each Parkston man a Sharps sawed off double barrel shotgun they had concealed. Alex carried the same gun, but Henry favored a sawed off 97 pump shotgun.

The hooligans turned to meet the foursome and Henry fired a warning shot into the air. It didn't stop them, the gruff looking men started after the smaller Moss. "He has a knife Henry!" Alex used his shotgun as a club and shattered the arm of the knifeman. Then, there was a loud whack as one of the attackers broke his bat over the massive back of Alex. McKenzie turned and uttered with a snarl, "is that all you got mate?" As the batter turned and tried to run away, Alex grabbed him by the collar, hoisting the squirming man high in the air, he hurled him into the attackers, knocking several of them to the ground. Jake joined the fray. Taking up the classic boxing stance, he used right and left jabs to knock men off balance, one down, then another. Finally, another blast from Henry's Winchester got some attention. "I have six left you sons of bitches, and my boys haven't spent any." Henry pumped his Winchester and it responded by sending another load of Pointers Prime buckshot from the magazine into the chamber.

Alex to Tommy, Jake to Henry, the men were literally back to back to cover every direction. "You're my eyes back there Jake, is the wagon back to the jail yet?"

"It is, and some deputies are coming out to help."

"Yea, I got some police coming out of the courthouse; that should do it for now!"

Seconds later Sheriff O'Rourke confronted his saviors. "Damn it Jake Balas, I never thought I'd be saying thanks to you, but I am."

"You're welcome Sheriff; by the way, did boxing those boys' ears remind you of anything, like maybe Omaha twenty years ago?"

"Yea, you beat me pretty bad that night, and from the looks of it, you can still box!"

The sheriff got instructions from the Judge Lucas McCann to take a cooling off delay of a couple hours. The hearing will reconvene at two o'clock. When that time arrived, a hundred troopers from Fort Dakota would line the street to keep peace.

After that announcement most of the crowd dispersed. The Parkston delegation gathered at the Four Leaf Clover for lunch. "How do you think this hearing will go Tommy? Do you think Taylor and Cobb have done everything they needed to do to win this?"

"After that excitement this morning I sure hope so! There is never a dull moment when Henry Moss is around!" Everyone gave the boys a hand for their bravery. "But, to answer your question Jake, yes. But they don't have to win it right now. This is just a preliminary hearing, all we have to do is present our case and get the judge to take it to trial. That is where things will get tough! This has all been very simple compared to what we will be up against at the trial. These people have money, enormous amounts of money, and they will do anything to get Ruth Wiseman off."

The Minnehaha County Courthouse was the greatest display of Victorian style architecture west of the Mississippi River. Much to the dismay of the hundreds who had gotten into the court room for the morning hearing, the main court room inside the building was now empty. The bailiff had cleared the room to prepare it for the afternoon hearing. The court room was large and brown. As you entered from the rear and faced the judge's bench some sixty feet to the front of the room, you would see, from left to right, three sections of seats. The first section contained sixty-six seats, the middle section contained ninety-six seats, and the last section on the right contained sixty-six seats. A small balcony contained another thirty seats for total of two hundred and fifty-eight. There is a brown oak railing about three feet high traversing the entire fifty foot width of the room. The railing, only a few feet from the front row of each section, allows the audience to be very intimate with the participants in the trial.

The dominating feature of the room is the ornate judge's bench. The bench rests high on an elevated platform some six feet above the rest of the room. The judge will look down to the jury box at his extreme left, then to the table where the defendant is seated, and finally to the table that will seat the prosecuting attorneys. Directly beneath him are the witness box and a small table in the center for the court reporter. In front of the defendant is a table that will be used for the evidence for and against that said defendant.

A crowd of five hundred people on the street anticipated the doors to swing open at one o'clock and when that did happen, it took only minutes for two hundred and twenty or so of those precious seats to be taken. Each of the lucky occupants smiled and laughed, some men lit celebratory cigars, much to the dismay of many young women whose virgin lungs would suck in the second hand smoke. The bailiff had roped off the front two rows of the middle section for the witnesses and the families of the defendant and the victim so the final sixty people, including Marion Campbell, Jake and Tommy, squeezed in to standing room only. The only instruction to them was not to tip over any of the spittoons!

At a quarter past one the bailiff began to bring evidence for the prosecution to the evidence table. The first items would be papers in folders marked exhibit one, then two and etcetera up to item number ten. Each time the bailiff left the room, the fortunate gallery members would strain to see what he was bringing to the table. Neither the defense team nor the district attorney's team was in the room yet so the audience had a good look at the bailiff's work. On his eleventh exit and subsequent entrance, the bailiff carried a tray across the room and placed it on the table. People strained to see what was on the tray but could not, for the tray was covered with a linen cloth. Murmurs throughout the room heightened when the bailiff delivered item number twelve, an exact replica of item eleven, a tray covered with a linen cloth. People again got up from their seats and strained to see what the man was doing at the table but couldn't as he had his back to them. Finally, one cloth was removed, folded and laid to the side. Then a second cloth was removed, folded and placed to the side. When the bailiff slowly turned and walked away, what he had uncovered left the crowd speechless. Two one gallon glass jars filled with formaldehyde stood on top of the evidence table. Exhibit number eleven contained Agnes Kreutzer's heart, and exhibit number twelve contained her brain!

The audience had been so enthralled by the delivery of the evidence that they didn't even notice the entrance of the lawyers and the defendant. Seated at the five foot by ten foot table in front of an empty jury box were Judge Acres and Ruth Wiseman. Seated directly behind them was Walter. Some prominent people of the city showed their support of the Wisemans with their presence including the mayor of Sioux Falls, James P. Bottoms and US Senator Phillip Opp.

District Attorney Leland Cobb's table was a little bit more crowded with Tony Taylor and Kirby Johnson. Vera Cobb occupied one of the seats in the reserved section behind the prosecutor along with other witnesses and family members. John and Christine were there with Grace. Henry Moss accompanied Lily and the girls to help represent the Kreutzer family. Witnesses included Vilas Sorenson, Ellie Rumbolz, Denton Noble, and Drs. Olsen and Paulson. Witnesses from Parkston included Dr. Hughes, Zachary Rothe, Ben Miller and Father Mullaney. Bumpers, who no one really knew what to do with was also present, seated nondescriptly behind the Wisemans.

The closer each tick of the large wall clock mounted behind the jury box took the stuffed room to the two o'clock start, the more nervous the atmosphere in the room became. The constant swish of hand held fans, smoke induced coughs and the occasional clang of a juicy wad of chew finding a spittoon were the only interruptions to the silence. Finally, with the temperature outside nearing one-hundred degrees, the bailiff ordered the five massive six foot wide by twelve foot high windows on the street side of the room thrown open in an effort to get some ventilation. It didn't help. Apparently the air pressure inside the room was greater than the air pressure outside so the room actually exhaled, sending smoke out the windows to the street. What this did accomplish however, was let thirty to forty street dwellers hug the open window sill and see what was happening inside. It also allowed flies and mosquitoes in to make things even more uncomfortable in the furnace like room.

At two o'clock sharp, the bailiff came out to make an unwelcome announcement to the sweaty crowd. "Judge Lucas McCann sends his apologies; we all know how uncomfortable it is in here, but, there will be a short delay of fifteen minutes or so. It seems the judge's gout has flared up in his right foot and he has, at the instruction of his doctor, been eating cherries. It should take only a few minutes for the soothing cherry juice to reach his swollen foot and quell the throbbing pain. I will keep you updated."

The crowd let out a collective moan and a few snickers. The humor broke the tension. Cobb nudged Tony, "A few minutes my ass," Leland chuckled, "as big as Lucas is it could take that juice all afternoon to find his right foot!"

Henry took this opportunity to excuse himself from Lily. He quietly shuffled past the front row where the witnesses for the state were seated and sat down in the empty chair reserved for Hubert. "Where in the hell is he Ellie? Good thing the judge delayed this for fifteen minutes."

Ellie seemed concerned. "I do not know. It is so unlike him to be this late. Whatever he is doing must be important. On the other hand Henry, that is kind of an odd couple over there isn't it?"

"Where?"

Ellie gestured toward the Nate Bumpers who had taken a seat next to Dr. Downing during this delay. "Did I tell you he was at the hospital that Friday afternoon?"

"Who, Bumpers?"

"Yes, I thought I told you that, anyway, look at how fidgety he is. He usually has that calm demeanor, confident to say the least! The only other time I have seen him that way was the Friday afternoon Agnes died, not the morning...just that afternoon. It is like he is waiting for something bad to happen...wishing whatever it was would just go away!"

Henry was confused. "Who are you talking about Ellie, Nate Bumpers?"

"I'm sorry, I was talking about...look Henry, here comes Hubert!"

Carrying a small envelope, Hubert Schnell hurried down the aisle and reached to shake Henry's hand. "I have great news. You know that box I delivered to Dr. Paulsen yesterday? It was Agnes's blood,

Denton saved it. Yes sir, he tested it and what he found is right here in this envelope. You have to get this to Tony, it could change everything!"

Henry took the packet and got Tony's attention, the DA came back to the railing, "What is going on back there Henry?"

"Tony, do you remember my theory about Agnes being drugged by Ruth?"

"I do, but I thought the doctors dispelled that after the autopsy?"

"They did, I did too. But we have new evidence here. It seems Denton kept the fluids after he embalmed Agnes to kind of cover his ass in case of trouble. He took the fluids to Paulsen's lab and here are the results. Now I'm going to tell you what we think happened and you take to Leland, ok?"

"No, save us some time and just get over to the table and tell both of us!"

Henry huddled at the table with Cobb for what seemed like forever to Hubert and Ellie. After three or four minutes, Tony got up and ran down the aisle to the rear door, grabbing Vera on the way out! Henry gave a wink and a smile to Hubert and Ellie as he passed them and then settled down beside Lily. He took her hand and gently squeezed it. "We caught that damn greased pig, now if we can just hang on!"

It was so quiet in the room you could almost hear Walter ask Frank Acres what was going on. When the bailiff would convene the court, Acres would ask for an explanation. For now, a single gong of the big clock on the wall told the over heated spectators it was two-thirty. The bailiff spoke.

"The Honorable Judge Lucas McCann, all rise."

A deputy of the court pushed the judge's wheelchair up to the bench nearly banging his wrapped gout foot into the side of it. "Sorry Judge, you usually you walk in on your own."

"Side bar if I could your Honor, Leland didn't have any time to waste as Tony and Vera had not returned yet. Ex-judge Acres joined the state counsel in front of the bench. Actually they had to go around to the side because the judge could not quite see all way down to them.

"What have I missed Leland? You should have had plenty of time with my delay."

"We have new evidence that is going to change the way the state will charge Ruth Wiseman. District Attorney Taylor is making those changes now Judge. We thought we would have them back here before you came out sir."

"Do you have any problem with this Frank?"

"No sir, not at this time." Acres should not oppose, the charges as of now were the most severe Ruth could get.

"How long do you anticipate this to take Leland...never mind, I see them back there."

Bang, bang, bang, went the gavel and the bailiff cried, "Order in the court, the preliminary hearing of the State of South Dakota versus Ruth Wiseman is now in session. Would the district attorney read the charges?"

Leland stood up and in a strong confident voice read the charges, "the state will prove that Ruth Wiseman did intentionally commit bodily harm to the victim Agnes Kreutzer and send her to the hospital in grave danger of dying. The charge will be voluntary and aggravated assault with the intent to commit said bodily harm!"

The audience was visibly upset. Where was the charge of murder? "We want the Jewess for murder" someone cried out.

"Order, order in my court. We can finish this in an empty room. If there is not quiet, I will clear you all out!" McCann was in no mood for games. "Side bar gentlemen. What is the intent here Leland? We have a dead girl and you are the one who started all of this by saying she was murdered. How do you intend to proceed?"

Leland cleared his throat. "We came across new evidence only this afternoon that sheds a different light on what we think happened. It seems Denton Noble saved the body fluids of the victim and they were tested over at the Methodist Hospital lab. The results just came to me. They will be admitted as evidence if you allow the state to conclude with Mrs. Wiseman, and then proceed with a new charge."

"Very well, we will proceed, but no surprises that will set this crowd off! Bailiff, please continue."

"The defendant will please rise. "How do you respond to the charge set before you?"

Acres responded, "Not guilty."

"The plea has been duly recorded and the bailiff will check my schedule and set a time for the trial. Now what is this other business you are talking about Leland? Please, approach the bench. Not you Frank, you are done. Mr. Acres, you may return to your seat. Leland and Taylor is it? You two may approach."

"It is very simple Lucas, same victim but a different set of charges against a different person. We are confident of our evidence and the person we intend to charge is in the room. If you would allow us, I would like to let Mr. Taylor read the charges. His team from Parkston did all of the work."

Judge McCann thought about a conflict of interest if two different people could be charged at the same preliminary hearing but his foot was still throbbing. "You may continue Mr. Taylor."

"Thank you your honor." Leland and Tony returned to the table and Tony picked up the paper he and Vera had so hurriedly typed up. I hope I have this right he thought to himself. Just as he was ready to step away from the table, Leland grabbed his arm, "good work boy," he whispered.

Taylor cleared his throat, "The state is indeed here to prosecute the murder of Agnes Kreutzer. We intend to do so at all cost. We have changed the charge against Ruth Wiseman because it will allow us to file a new charge for Agnes. That charge is, PREMEDITATED MURDER IN THE FIRST DEGREE AGAINST DOCTOR CALVIN DOWNING!!!"

The crowd roared and leaped to their feet as Downing slumped forward in his chair. He was sitting just behind and to the left of where the Wisemans and Frank were. After a few seconds Downing went to the railing behind Frank Acres. "Frank, you have to help me Frank!"

"I can't help you now Calvin. I have Ruth and Walter here."

There was so much activity and noise in the room no one really saw Calvin slip inside the railing and beg Acres for his help. Downing looked to Walter. "Can you help me Walter?"

Walter looked his old friend in the eye and saw the fear. "You killed Agnes didn't you Calvin? Why?"

Downing, with sweaty palms down on the table, stiffened his slumped shoulders and stood erect in response to Walter's question. "Why you ask?" Downing was oblivious to the fact that the judge, the bailiff and the deputies were getting the crowd in order; the room was quiet as he spoke. "Why did I kill her? I did it for you Walter, you know that."

"Calvin, shut up. You don't have to do this!" Frank had no success quieting his friend.

Calvin was in a trance, or else he simply did not care that everyone in the room could hear what he was saying. "I took care of that beaten girl just like all the other girls Ruth mishandled when she was drunk. Only this was worse. She beat that child within an eyelash of death. She should have finished the job, but she didn't. Ruth just called on old Doctor Downing to save the day. When I saw the girl at the hospital that afternoon, I knew she would live. Don't you see Walter, this one would have talked. You couldn't buy this one like you did all the others. So I got the nurse to leave on a wild goose chase and I filled a syringe with heroine and injected it in her. Then I put that syringe in my pocket and when the nurse returned with my bag, I gave the girl another injection. I knew that much would kill her. She just closed her eyes and went to sleep, never to sing again. I did it all for you Walter, don't you understand?"

THE END